The Amazing F

England to India With Strangers

Apinder Sahni

The Amazing Road Trip Home – England to India With Strangers

Copyright © by Apinder Sahni.

The right of Apinder Sahni to be identified as the author of this Work has been asserted by him in accordance with the Copyright, Designs and Patents Act 1988.

All rights reserved. No part of this book may be reproduced in any form by electronic means, stored in a retrieval system, or transmitted, in any form or by any other means, without written permission from the author, except for the use of brief quotations in a book review.

This book was first published in February 2022, by

Apinder Sahni.

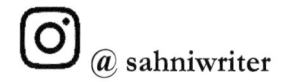

@ sahniwriter

Cover design by Hyde Panesar

www.beardboydesign.com

ISBN: 978-1-80068-496-6

Independent Publishing Network

Prologue 1

England opened her arms 7

The moment has arrived 11

7 months before the road trip 16

6 months before the road trip 25

1963 - An opportunity from England 30

5 months before the road trip 33

1963 - A simple formula: £1 = Rs13 41

4 months before the road trip 44

3 ½ months before the road trip 52

1963 - The conversation 57

3 months before the road trip 60

2 ½ months before the road trip 69

1963 - The Invite 74

1 month before the road trip 77

1963 - A giant leap of faith 82

1 week before the road trip 86

Leaving Slough for Dover 90

1963 - A different sun and smell 93

To Dover and across 96

Paris here we come 102

1963 - Being brave 107

Let's sample some of Paris 111

Sometimes, we can be too trusting 117

1963 - Let fate take me 124

Bye Paris, hello Switzerland 127

An old acquaintance 135

1963 - New faces and places 140

West Germany and camping 145

The ice between the passengers begins to break 152

Austria the ice capped beauty 160

1963 - Finding His Feet 171

1963 – Faith and patience pay off 174

Salzburger Nockel, an Austrian delicacy 178

A chance meeting 186

Brief, but a taste of home 193

1964 - Integration underway 205

1964 – Something else is brewing 211

It gets rocky in Yugoslavia 213

Is this the end of the road? 221

The Police station 224

Thankful to leave the jungle, in one piece 234

1964 - Love develops 241

It's getting dusty 244

It's not just the car that needs repairs 253

Going through cold Turkey 257

The reality of the road kicks in 262

Time to connect, with faith and a friend 269

Barriers begin to fall, the mystery clears 277

1964 - A new face? 284

1964 - It's decision time 288

A prized asset no more 291

1964 - Held by a thin thread 300

1965 – Mind made up 304

Austin, we must depart 306

1965 - Now there were two 314

The Motherland is on the horizon 318

1965 – Blue envelope 324

1966 – Gurcharan finds his feet 326

1966 – Time for a new home 332

1967 – Where did the time go since landing? 334

One road trip ends, another journey begins 337

We're here, so time for change 344

Search for a partner starts 350

Some things are just meant to be 354

Mission complete 359

Beyond the Road 362

Firmly cemented in England 367

Epilogue 375

Acknowledgments 379

Timeline 383

Inder's Voucher for England 384

Morris Austin Cambridge Estate 385

Gurdwara on 79 Sinclair Road, Shepherd Bush 386

Gurcharan and Charanjit with family 387

Happy couples 388

Returning home after the road trip 389

Petersfield Avenue 390

Late Inder Singh Chhatwal 391

Bibliography 392

About the Author 393

Prologue

I was fortunate that, growing up my parents had a very active social life. Like so many immigrants, they moved to England in the 1970s in search of a better future. As they carefully adopted to the British way of life, little time was wasted in making friends with other immigrant families. You would become acquainted with a family, who would then introduce you to their friends. Bound by duty you'd fittingly reciprocate with introductions to your friends. The entire process was driven through word of mouth and that's how the network of extended friends and families grew. New relationships were forged and bound together for the foreseeable future.

The weekend would arrive, and this meant a gathering of some kind. My parents were always mindful of their social circle, and keen on one which promoted equality of conversations. They were far removed from the idea that men and women should sit separately. During these social gatherings, everyone would take the opportunity to showcase their skills. Some would bring cooked food with them. Pakoras (onion bhajee's) and samosas that would make a crisp crunching noise as you bit into them. The mouth-watering main courses came filled with an aroma of spices. My mum would make steamed rice and hot chapati's to accompany these. As the evening relaxed to a slumber, some would sing or share poetry. These were beautiful memories growing up that taught me an invaluable lesson in life. The first-generation of Indians moving to Britain had so much more to offer in addition to their hard-working ethic. Beyond the long hours, and when time allowed, they possessed talents in art, music and prose. But nothing had prepared me for what I was about to discover later in my life.

It was 2016, and I'd heard of a local resident who embarked on a road trip from Gravesend (in Kent) to India, to raise money for charity. During one of our weekend gatherings, I happened to mention this feat to some relatives. It came as a huge surprise when two of my uncles commented that they had made a similar road trip. All these years and no one had ever mentioned this. A smile that could reach both ends of my ears beamed across my face, and I wanted to know more. A few days later I contacted both my uncles, the Chhatwal brothers, to at least rekindle some of those memories. My phone conversation with them was brief but it was the question they both posed to me that got me thinking. **Who would be interested in our journey?** This was the perfect motivation I needed to get writing.

It was a Saturday morning in December, and unusually bright. I noticed the dew settling on the grass, as I peered into my garden. In front of me, the dining table was well prepared with a plate of hot samosas, a bowl of green chutney and a good mix of biscuits. I had invited Inder and Gurcharan Singh Chhatwal to my house to discover what drove them to embark on a journey of such magnitude. Truth be told I was nervous and not sure what to expect, or whether my preparation was any good to help capture our discussions. So many years had passed, would they remember much? A few hours into our conversations I discovered how wrong I was. Their faces gleamed, and their eyes were full of joyful tears during an afternoon spent in memories. Their recall of detail some forty years on was astonishing.

Following many months of interviewing, I felt like a passenger on this epic journey. It was even more special considering the brothers didn't have a single photo for any part of the trip. This was a journey which took them across nine countries and twenty-one days to complete. What makes their adventure even more amazing, is that before this, they had never driven out of London.

Inder and Gurcharan Singh Chhatwal were part of the first generation of Indian immigrants who left their home and loved ones in search of work. They came to England for a better life. Unselfish and relentless hard work enabled them to send money back home to their extended families. However, the brothers also had a sense of adventure about them. You will see how Inder and Gurcharan's early years in England demonstrated their determination, pragmatism and belief in their faith. It is these characteristics that enabled them to embark on the precarious journey to India.

I do hope this story will be a tangible reminder to them of their great adventure. A reference for their families, and an insight to us all of what a real adventure is. But this book travels beyond the road trip, and speaks of the key events that led the brothers making this journey to England in the first instance.

To my father. I wish I could have written your journey.

To my mother, whose journey I can't wait to write.

England opened her arms

The impact of World War II left Britain with a tough rebuilding headache. Labour shortages within its own country meant a fast track route was needed to recruit a new workforce. Inder and Gurcharan Singh Chhatwal were 9 and 6 years old respectively when the British Nationality Act of 1948 was passed in Parliament. This was the open-door invitation to its Commonwealth subjects.

No sooner had the news reached the shores of Britain's Commonwealth countries, people started arriving in their droves. A period of mass migration was marked by the symbolic arrival of the SS Empire Windrush from Kingston, Jamaica to Tilbury in June 1948. It was reported some five hundred West Indians arrived with the intention of starting new lives.

The number of Indian migrants was relatively low around this time. But it wouldn't take long for that to change. Prior to that, West Indians bore the brunt of adjusting to a new country. While their past heroics were applauded in Parliament, the treatment was very much different amongst the British public. Simply put, immigrants were not welcomed in their country.

Accommodation was restricted, and there were often notices stating *no coloured people*. This was not common practice, but some landlords sighted fear of reprisal from white neighbours as reason for this behaviour.

The author Robert Winder, in his book **Bloody Foreigners – The Story of Immigration To Britain** - states that when it came to council housing, Jamaicans were *at the back of the queue*. In some cases, where West Indians had the financial means to acquire a mortgage, banks saw them as a *bad risk* and refused.

The sheer weight of mass immigration was being felt around the country. The Notting Hill Riots of 1958 saw large outbreaks of violence. Fighting between black and white people resulted in shops and homes being severely damaged.

The situation left the country in limbo. They couldn't put immigration on hold for fear of being seen to discriminate. But they had to stem the influx of numbers and do it fast. In 1961 the British government introduced the work permit scheme for entry into the country. You would now be accepted entry based on:

(1) those with job offers.
(2) those with credible skills or qualifications.
(3) quota for those with none of the above.

Indians rallied over from all parts of India, Panjab, Pakistan and Bangladesh. By 1955 there were some 5000 Indians living in Britain[1]. Settling into industries such as textiles and manufacturing, they worked hard to establish themselves. Two years later this figure jumped to just under 7000.

The work permit scheme only stemmed the flow slightly. Britain's next move to further tighten the process, was the Commonwealth Immigrants Act of

---

[1] National Archives website – Bound for Britain

1962. For those who were already settled in Britain, life did not get any easier. It was Britain who had invited the people of the Commonwealth and so they felt like it was also their home. But to their shock they were considered outsiders by the white locals, and so began a challenging journey.

The moment has arrived

It had been a restless day for Inder and Gurcharan, and tomorrow they would embark on the first leg of their road trip to India. In their sheer excitement they had packed days ago, making sure nothing was missed out. However, they couldn't suppress the lingering thoughts in their minds about this trip. What if they didn't make it all the way? They hadn't really discussed any fall-back options; it had been full steam ahead in terms of planning. But the Chhatwal brothers always had a positive outlook on life, and were looking forward to taking on a challenge.

Chanan Singh had sensed the slight tension in the house, and took some action. In true Indian tradition he organised a small farewell party for the brothers. As the evening arrived, a table was pitched in the small room at the front of the hallway. It was filled with a variety of dishes cooked by the landlord's wife. Everyone took it in turns to fill up their plates with the delicious, spicy food. The aroma of the cooked spinach, mixed vegetables and minced lamb filled the air, masking any trepidation. The hot chapattis were consumed in numbers and quick succession. Inder and Gurcharan were mindful that it could be a while before they tasted any home cooked food again.

Helping their friends clean up, the occupants of the house pleaded with the brothers to explain the route one last time. Due to a much-needed change in mood, excitement now rightly dominated the brother's faces. With beaming smiles etched across their faces, they spoke of countries which most of the household members had never heard of. Holding up a large colourful map, Inder gleefully showed the proposed route, with the audience following attentively. The brothers raised their eyebrows as it dawned on them the number of countries and scale of land mass they had to cover.

Before retiring to bed, they moved their luggage into the hallway near the front door. The daily routine meant occupants of the house waking up early for work however, the brothers would be the first to leave the next morning. Hugs were exchanged, blessings bestowed, and for a moment, Inder and Gurcharan were back in India. It was just like the day before they each left to come to England. That same feeling in the stomach; the fear of the unknown. Tomorrow they would meet the passengers for whom they were responsible for driving to India. Glancing at each other, the brothers hoped there would be plenty of harmony along the way.

As the clock signalled 4:00am, both sprung from their beds as normal and groomed themselves like they did every day. With beards tied neatly, turbans wrapped tightly, and a brew of homemade Indian tea consumed, the brothers sat crossed legged on the lounge floor. As if in perfect harmony and synchronisation, both started reciting the morning Sikh prayer, Japji Sahib[2]. This was a daily routine which they carried out with full attention, but today they were consumed more than

---

[2] The Japji Sahib is a sacred hymn which can be found at the beginning of the Sikh Holy book, the Guru Granth Sahib Ji. It was composed by the first Guru, Sri Guru Nanak Dev Ji and gives a comprehensive essence of Sikhism.

ever. At the end of the prayer they partook in the Ardas (Sikh prayer to close worship) and proceeded to wait patiently.

It was very early and sparing a thought for the sleeping neighbours, there wouldn't be a horn to signal the arrival of their passengers. Inder was the first to spot the Austin Cambridge. He signalled to Gurcharan and they carefully made their way to the hallway, opened the front door and walked out with their luggage. The weary looking man greeted them with a handshake, then swiftly moved away. He signalled to the space left on the roof rack for their luggage and helped them position it carefully. An additional strap was handed to Gurcharan, so that their luggage could be securely locked in. The man then made his way to the back seat of the car to join the rest of his family. Inder had the pleasure of starting off the driving, with Gurcharan navigating.

As they both perched themselves in the front, they turned to introduce each other to the man's wife and his son. The exchange was brief; a simple nod. She was dressed in traditional Indian attire, with her hair tied back neatly and a tired expression across her face. Their son was sleeping silently, no doubt playing catch up having been disturbed so early from his slumber.

Before starting the car, there was a momentary but silent exchange between Inder and Gurcharan. They were both thinking the same thing. Had they suddenly underestimated this road trip, the enormity of what they were about to embark on?

With a small blessing ushered under their breath, Inder started the car and they headed towards Dover. It was Wednesday 4th October 1967.

7 months before the road trip

Inder and Gurcharan had been in England for a couple of years and were adjusting to the British way of life. It was a complete leap of faith, that the brothers had stepped into a country alien to them. Very little was known of England, or what the people were like but to this point they had trusted their instincts to survive. Their minds often wondered back to the days each left for England. Some of the locals had spoken of English streets lined with detached houses and huge gardens. A country where there was plenty of food to go around, and all the children were plump.

Inder and Gurcharan couldn't speak for the rest of the country, but living in West London, it wasn't all lush gardens and large houses. Then there was the weather and its ability to churn out all four seasons in a single month. They found the changes in weather so rapid that it sometimes left them bemused. Recalling one morning, the sun had shone bright and the brothers wore light clothing on their daily commute. No sooner had they hopped off the bus, the sun disappeared, and a mini monsoon left them drenched.

Nonetheless, it had been a testing time and adjustment came at the price of hard work and diligence. Yes, they were young but knew full well the risks they had taken to come to England. Regardless, they didn't feel despondent, but rather upbeat that this decision would be a fruitful one.

The yearning to see their family towered over them like an endless shadow refusing to leave. The more they embedded themselves into work and life, meant a step further away from the possibility of seeing their loved ones. The urge to visit home was growing, and it would certainly help re-assure any insecurities that all was going well.

The last few letters and calls left the brothers a little dejected. There was a sadness that had started creeping into the mood back home. Like so many others in their position, the brothers depended heavily on those very letters from loved ones. They had witnessed first-hand what it was like when there was no communication with those left behind. Only last year one of the occupants in the house stopped receiving letters and his world seemed to collapse. It was those words of comfort that maintained the bond, and the reason some of them battled each day.

It wasn't until recently that their sister had mustered up the courage to ask them whether they were coming back home at all. Her question came as a surprise, but they understood her concern. It was a question on the tip of everyone's tongue, the question which held those awkward silences on the phone. It then dawned on the brothers that there was no option of holding out any longer. Whatever timeline they had set themselves, it was no longer justifiable.

Something didn't seem right. Money was reaching back home as planned, ensuring the family had more than enough cover for daily essentials. Inder and Gurcharan had very little left for themselves, but that didn't matter to them. The maturity each carried ensured both remained focused on the objective.

They set themselves a target of visiting home very soon, even if for a brief while. Their first port of call was to visit a travel agent in Slough with a view of obtaining the cost of flights. Some of housemates recommended a travel agency run by an Indian man who was renowned for competitive prices. While this was true, the reality was Indian immigrants, such as the housemates, felt intimidated walking into a shop full of white people. Regardless of how long they had been here, plucking up the courage to do that was an impossible feat at present.

Opting for a weekend when there wasn't any overtime on offer, the brothers headed into the high street to make their enquiry. Walking in they noticed the tight space of the shop. There was a large wooden desk at the back piled with folders and paperwork. A faded chair, with a thick coat hanging off it meant someone was around. Inder shuffled his feet, and the sound seemed to spark some movement from the back office. A plump, bearded gentleman walked out with a cup of tea, whose fragrance of cardamom consumed the office.

The point from which the brothers nestled into the chairs to them briskly walking out lasted all but fifteen minutes. Two glum looking faces emerged back out with shoulders drooping and heads bent down. They hadn't anticipated the cost of flights being as expensive as what they were told. To make matters worse, the travel agent had assured them it would still be the most competitive price anywhere in town. The cost was now a huge sticking point for them both.

What was more concerning, was that purchasing even one ticket would prove a challenge. Whatever they earned was split between a portion sent home and their accommodation. Even the savings they had were insufficient to fund a ticket. Combined, their efforts left them with very little each week. A quick calculation revealed it could take at least six months just to be able to purchase one ticket.

The travel agent had also told them that prices often fluctuated depending on when they were travelling. This could prove another headache if work was not flexible enough in granting leave. That bombshell of information pretty much added to their misery. As always, they decided to seek advice from their trusted friend Chanan Singh.

Evening approached and everyone in the house gathered around for their meal. Sitting together and eating had become an important ritual for everyone. The dialog ranged from what happened at work, local and national news and guidance on personal matters. When the food was consumed, Inder and Gurcharan shared their desire to visit home.

Chanan Singh was the only member of the house who had travelled back to India since arriving in England, and this was for his own wedding. The cost of that trip had been jointly funded by his own parents and prospective in-laws. This, he said feeling rather ashamed, formed part of the dowry that was customary within Indian families. The mere mention of the ticket price caused anguished looks on some faces, followed by the odd profanity in Panjabi. It was a tall order to purchase just the one ticket, and the disappointment reverberated around the room.

All the housemates could see that the brothers were desperate to go back, and so offered to contribute some money from their own savings towards a ticket. The kind gesture was declined by Inder and Gurcharan. As much as they appreciated the show of kindness, it wasn't a problem they felt the housemates had to resolve at their own expense. The brothers knew too well that they would never be hassled to return the money any time soon. However, considering all those variables, they had faith that an opportunity would present itself somewhere.

Several weeks had passed since the travel agent episode, and the brothers continued to apply themselves in daily work and study. Their wage continued to cater for basic needs and a small contribution towards home improvements. Over the past few years, the rent had remained significantly low, and so they felt compelled to help in the upkeep of their shared residence.

In the meantime, phone calls to family were becoming shorter and less frequent. Inder and Gurcharan kept avoiding any conversations about when they were visiting. It wasn't that their family would be ashamed or think any less of them. Inder was more mindful of what the locals in their neighbourhood would be thinking. Their father was a proud man however, such was the mentality within the community that many may have started pointing fingers. Had Surjan Singh's sons not returned yet? Did they not care for the welfare of elderly parents and their unmarried sister? Such negative comments and back chat were commonplace in tight knit communities.

Chanan Singh could see the gradual decline in the brother's demeanour, and they had not been themselves for a while. It was therefore decided, despite their reluctance, that the brothers would now take up the generous offer presented to them by the housemates. One return ticket would be purchased for that visit back home. Who would go was still up for discussion, and this was largely dependent on which one of them could get time off work.

Inder and Gurcharan were both well settled in their respective jobs and had good relationships with their line managers. But the fact remained, any sustained absence from work could act against them. As genuine as friendships may have seemed, they were non-white. A coloured group of workers with the task of being as productive as possible without asking too many questions. There were hundreds like them fresh from the homeland waiting in line, looking on for even the smallest of opportunities to take their place.

At least for now there was hope in their hearts and they could start planning the short visit home. Inder and Gurcharan shopped around for a ticket. They could easily have returned to the same travel agent but, seeing someone else was paying, the least they could do was exert some effort into finding the very best price. With a helping hand from friends they could see some light at the end of the tunnel.

6 months before the road trip

It was a Sunday morning as the brothers lazily made their way to the kitchen for some tea. They had almost forgotten what it felt like not having to rush off to work on a weekend, as recently things had been relentless. Their efforts had been split between working the usual hours and overtime. When time allowed, they'd visit travel agencies for flight deals.

As a change of scenery, both wanted to take a walk around the more suburban part of where they lived. Large detached houses on the other side of the high street often gave birth to aspirations. Before venturing out, Gurcharan grabbed the local newspaper resting on the side table, to see what was happening in the area. In fact, the brothers were the only ones in the house who ever read the newspaper. It provided them with an insight into the local community, and was essential for integration they felt.

Whenever the opportunity allowed itself, Inder would acquire a copy of the Slough Observer from work at the end of the week. No one questioned it, and no one really bothered reading it either. The white employees seemed engrossed in reading a newspaper called *The Sun*. Inder didn't take much interest in that publication and a copy never made it home with him.

Flicking through, Gurcharan was most interested in the classified section. These were several pages awash with used items for sale and local services on offer. The adverts were small, squashed in a box, and required careful scanning to determine their relevance. Such items included clothes, toys, carpets, cars, and general household goods. There was even someone offering to read your future.

On numerous instances Gurcharan had wanted to enquire about items on sale. Yet he never picked up the phone. His reluctance stemmed from a preconception about the voice on the other end. No doubt the person would be English, and maybe on hearing his accent would refuse to sell him the item? Until someone plucked up the courage, they would never know.

As Gurcharan scanned the list, he noticed a posting that stood out from the rest. It was an advert in bold letters reading **Wanted! Two gentlemen to drive a car from Slough to India**. Gurcharan called out to Inder, as he didn't trust his own eyes. Inder took the newspaper from Gurcharan and placed it carefully on the small side table. He read the advert to himself, then did so again, this time loud so Gurcharan could hear.

The first thought that popped into their heads was why would anyone want to drive to India. Scrolling down, Inder noticed the name on the advert, which sounded Indian. However, he couldn't be certain. Often immigrant workers adopted English sounding names in favour of their traditional ones. The adoption wasn't by choice, but rather thrust upon them. Inder had once quizzed a co-worker on his nickname, to which the response was blamed on fitting in.

The truth of the matter was the same white co-workers struggled with pronouncing ethic names, and they didn't want to try. Johnny, it seemed was quite popular, often a replacement for *Jatinder* or *Jagdish*. Before taking any decision on this advert, the brothers felt compelled in consulting Chanan Singh.

Later that evening, Chanan Singh, Inder and Gurcharan discussed the advert. Chanan Singh remained pragmatic, airing on the side of caution. He pointed out the potential dangers of travelling such a long distance by road. In comparison, the brothers' emotional state crept in as they sighted the opportunity to visit home. While none of them had any idea of the route, Inder and Gurcharan's minds were already swirling with the excitement of travelling across different countries. It seemed they were already on the road.

A reluctant Chanan Singh finally gave his blessing but, on the condition that the brothers write to their family back home and gain their permission. This of course was the natural step, but the brothers weren't going to wait that long. They promised they would write, but not before dialling the number to see whether this was indeed the stroke of luck they were hoping for.

1963 - An opportunity from England

Inder and Gurcharan were born in the city of Hoshiarpur, north-east of Panjab. Their other siblings included three brothers and a sister. Within the community they were regarded as a respectable family who worked hard to maintain a modest lifestyle. Never one to be ashamed of his position, it didn't bother their father one bit that they didn't own a home. They lived in rented accommodation because their father had decided a long time ago not to take the risk of borrowing money.

Now in their early 20s, Inder worked as a draughtsman and Gurcharan as an engineer. Although both of their personal lives were progressing well, they often felt there was little chance of climbing out from the circle of rented accommodation. While there was never any pressure to go above and beyond their jobs, a sense of responsibility loomed large on their conscious to make major changes.

It was early morning in January, and a close friend of Inder's rushed in through the front door. Luckily for Varinder, the door was wide open, a practice synonymous with majority of households who felt secure. Tucked tightly under his arm was a fresh copy of The Tribune newspaper. On seeing Inder and Gurcharan's father he fell silent, clasped his hands and uttered **Sat Sri Akhal Ji[3] Papaji[4]**. *He walked past and proceeded on greeting their mother by respectively touching her feet.*

Before their father could offer him a cup of tea, Varinder quickly vanished in search of the brothers. On finding Inder, he sat him down, unfolded the newspaper and showed him an advert that he hoped would change their fortunes. The advert, taking up half a page was written in both English and Panjabi. The thick black border around it aimed to single out its importance.

It was an invitation to members of the Commonwealth to apply for a working visa to England. Inder ushered over Gurcharan and asked him to have a look at the advert, and then both stared at each other. A brief discussion took place on whether this was something worth proceeding. Varinder could see the brothers were eager, he knew that from the onset. But he was also quietly aware of the potential implications of applying. If

---

[3] Sat(truth) Sri(great) Akhal(timeless being) is a Sikh greeting in Panjabi.
[4] A reference of respect for someone elder than yourself, fatherly figure

successful, this meant an opportunity to work abroad. Inder's mind had already planted itself in the seat of the airplane waiting for take-off. However, he noticed Gurcharan didn't quite have the same enthusiasm.

Bubbling with excitement, Inder asked Gurcharan why he looked sombre. Looking straight back at him, Gurcharan reminded his brother that someone would have to bring up the subject with their father.

5 months before the road trip

From the moment Inder and Gurcharan awoke, their minds were preoccupied with the advert in the Slough Observer. No doubt others would have seen it too. Before leaving for work, Gurcharan contemplated calling in sick. He was eager to call the number on the advert. However, he knew such short notice would cause great inconvenience at his workplace.

As each moment passed, they became nervous at the thought of missing this opportunity. It was no surprise when the working day finished, that both made their way home as quick as possible. The first course of action was to make that call. Tea and snacks were put on hold while Gurcharan and Inder left the house for the telephone box.

The rosso red telephone box stood like a beacon of hope to many immigrants. A portal to what now seemed a different world which they once called home. This was not their regular spot but further away.

However, this meant a good chance it wouldn't be occupied and so they wouldn't be queuing for their turn. Gurcharan opened the door and stepped in, while trying not to focus on the cards inside offering services of the shady kind. Inder followed suit, shutting the door behind him. Their slim profile allowing them both to stand without any discomfort.

Now perched up inside, Inder carefully held up the advert while Gurcharan picked up the receiver. He then dipped his hand into his pocket and reclaimed some coins to insert into the holding slot. Dialling the number ever so slowly, he waited for the ringing tone. Inder edged closer to Gurcharan so that he could listen in. With heartbeats racing, the anticipation of waiting ended with the phone being answered after a brief cough. Gurcharan pressed the button on the phone box so he could be heard too. The voice on the other end sounded mature and very British.

It was the fourth *hello* that sprung Gurcharan into life to get his words out. Trying to sound confident, he introduced himself, mentioning the advert in the local paper for two drivers. The voice on the other end introduced himself as Roy Chauhan. Without a moment's hesitation, he probed Gurcharan with some initial questions. Did he hold a driving licence? How much driving experience did he have? Gurcharan responded in a positive manner but was not sure if this satisfied Roy's questioning.

Gurcharan also mentioned his background as a mechanical engineer to add further weight, and to slow the stream of questions. This seemed to have worked and there was an awkward pause. Gurcharan could have sworn he heard Roy mumbling to himself. Inder made a gesture to ask Roy if he had had much response to his advert. In response Roy commented it was *early days*.

A brief hesitation hung in the air while Roy again mumbled to himself. Gurcharan was becoming conscious that he was running short on time, and before long more coins would have to be dispensed into the phone box. This call was beginning to turn into an agonising experience. Just as hope was fading, and

Gurcharan anticipating the end of the call, Roy proposed to call them back in two days' time.

The brothers looked bemused, and Inder wasn't sure how that went. The conversation sounded positive, but Roy wanted to ring them back. He could have asked them to call him, so did this mean he wasn't so sure on the brothers? Had the opportunity slipped from their grasp? Roy took note of the telephone number from where they were calling and agreed on a time.

There was much discussion in the house regarding the call. An air of uncertainty loomed as to whether this was going to lead to a successful outcome. This was certainly a view shared by the brothers if they were being honest with themselves. Chanan Singh remained upbeat and tried to inject some positivity. He addressed any fears they had by telling them that anyone considering this opportunity would have similar constraints.

There was the question of time off work and having the relevant experience. He was confident their personalities would give them the upper hand over any competitors. This was one of the many facets admired by everyone of Chanan Singh, he always found the positive in situations and understood the mood of his friends so well.

The housemates assured Inder and Gurcharan that regardless of the outcome, their offer to help finance a plane ticket still stood. Echoing the wise words of their forefathers, they advised them not to worry about a situation they had no control over. Even after their brief conversation, it was hard to ascertain what Roy was like as a person. He might genuinely have been interested, or he could have been making general talk to usher them away.

A few days later, and has agreed, Inder and Gurcharan walked back to the red telephone box, reaching ten minutes ahead of the scheduled time. The booth was empty, but Gurcharan was only too aware it could quickly be circled by eager immigrants wanting to call home. He stepped inside and kept his hand on the receiver, while Inder stood outside.

Inder wasn't a shy character, or one to distance himself from responsibility, but he let Gurcharan take the lead on the conversations. His brother had the engineering background and was very confident with technical questions.

Moments later another Indian man approached the telephone box. Inder knocked on the window to inform Gurcharan. He picked up the receiver to pretend he was on a call. Inder turned to face the stranger, shrugged his shoulders and rolled his eyes. He explained that the person in the booth had been there for some time. Then he let slip a white lie, that his call was to family back home and going to take a long while. The man pondered for a moment, turned and then headed in the opposite direction. For a moment the brothers were like kids again, playing pranks on others.

When the coast was clear, Gurcharan ushered Inder into the telephone box. They now waited with anticipation for the phone call, constantly glancing at their watches. The phone didn't ring at the agreed time. As each second passed the nervousness began to work its way into their stomachs. Seconds turned into minutes. In fact, it was the longest five minutes they had ever experienced. The question now was whether they hold out a bit longer or head back home.

Just then, the sound of the phone bellowed into the confined space. A loud long ring followed a momentary pause followed by another loud ring. This was on the verge of being one of the most significant calls they might ever receive. Gurcharan picked up the receiver and before he could utter any words, Roy Chauhan swiftly apologised for the lateness.

Gurcharan nodded with a smile to Inder as to indicate that it was a smart move to have waited. Roy recommended a face to face meeting at a café on the High Street. It was one not too far from where the brothers were living.

An early morning time was agreed and with that, he ended the call. They slipped out of the telephone box, and a huge sigh of relief washed over them. For a moment it was looking like a big disappointment heading in their direction. All those hopes they had built up suddenly being dashed away in an instant.

For now, that was not the case and this meeting provided another opportunity to impress. As they both walked back in the direction of home, Gurcharan spoke up. He had a seed of doubt, still, as to whether all this was too good to be true.

1963 - A simple formula: £1 = Rs13

A few days had passed since the conversation about the advert for a working visa. Inder was eager to share this potential opportunity with someone else in the family, and therefore turned to his sister, Swarn Kaur. On a practical level it was easy to see what an opportunity like this could mean for the whole family. If he could get a vote of confidence from his sister, then this would help with any tricky conversations. Inder was only too mindful that emotions could run high in such situations, and that's why his sister's support was of vital importance.

Swarn Kaur was sitting on the veranda when Inder approached her. Carrying the newspaper behind his back, his cheeks were red and eyes gleaming, the radiance of which could light up a dark room. He showed her the advert and then remained quiet for a moment. She remained silent, but then followed up with a comment to suggest that it sounded like a good opportunity. Without hesitation, Inder pressed ahead with what this could mean for them all. There was the obvious financial benefit; working in England provided the opportunity of doubling, and even tripling what he earnt now. Then there was the experience he would gain from working in a foreign country.

She was trying to follow his lead and to see the bigger picture. Inder took a different approach; that every pound earned in England amounted to thirteen rupees. That meant even the most manual of jobs in England paid more than high positions in their city. He pleaded with his sister that her support was important if he was to approach their father and discuss this opportunity.

Sardar Surjan Singh Chhatwal was a stout man of strong principals who loved his children dearly. He appreciated the efforts they all put in to ensure the family could make ends meet. His expectations never sought to put pressure on any member of the family. However, having lived in rented accommodation for the majority of their lives, he knew that Inder and Gurcharan had a burning desire to make changes. He had an inkling something was in the air but couldn't put his finger on it. For so long he had dismissed any such discussions about change, especially one's which could threaten the harmony of the family. If owning his own home meant a disruption to this balance, then he would rather make do with what they had. But little did Surjan Singh know that his principals were about to be challenged. This opportunity that promised potential new dreams had landed in the lap of one of his sons and was going to test a father's love.

4 months before the road trip

It was important they made the right impression. Gurcharan had taken on the job to wash their turbans, dry and carefully iron them with exceptional precision. Their turbans were made of thin material, and were 100% cotton, which meant you would apply steam to straighten out the creases. Gurcharan then placed them at the top of the cupboard, showing his utmost respect.

There was never a quiet weekend in the house, and the noise of footsteps and clattering of dishes in the kitchen meant housemates were up early for work. Attention now turned to their beards, which needed to be tied. When not groomed, the beards were free flowing, reaching just below the neck. This look was for home only, not when they went out, and by personal choice.

The brothers took turns in using the small bathroom, carefully applying a gel like substance called Fixo[5]. Back home this was the only go to product for them. A bright blue bottle with an orange sticker, the substance was dark brown and felt like thick glue on the hand. It had a strong smell to it, like correction fluid, which worked its way up the nostrils as you applied it.

When the gel was evenly applied, a thin cloth was wrapped around the chin and knotted at the top of the head. It was time to dry the beard. The thin cloth had two objectives; keep the beard pressed in tight and act as a barrier when drying. For Gurcharan and Inder, their beards were one of the most important aspects of their appearance. Each time the result had to be neat with not a single strand of hair out of place. Fixo guaranteed one thing in abundance, a very firm hold. Only a small amount of time was needed for drying, making the overall process efficient as possible.

Back home, they noticed a downside from overuse of the Fixo product, with close relatives sharing their experiences. There would come a point where elderly relatives decided on reducing the use of Fixo. Leaving

---

[5] Fixo is the short name given to a beard fixer gel which is commonly used in India by Sikh men

the beard to flow freely and allowing a natural transition to grey. However, what appeared was a colour that could only be described as a cross between yellow and aubergine. This slowed down the transition to going grey, leaving the recipient in limbo and feeling embarrassed. It seemed, the cocktail of strong, unknown ingredients in the Fixo product was to blame for this transformation. Did everyone using it suffer the same fate? Maybe not but it was worth the risk to gain that ultimate hold throughout the day.

The final jewel in the crown was to tie the perfect turban. From a young age their father had taught them about the importance of it. Often, he would stand watching each of his sons tie it, making sure the cloth did not touch the floor. ***This turban is the crown on your head*** he would tell them. Finally, they were ready, and it was time to set off.

A busy morning had masked the nerves bubbling on the surface. Gurcharan and Inder were venturing out to meet a total stranger in response to his advert. Having absolutely no idea about this man's intensions, a layer of uncertainty floated under the exterior.

It was a warm morning when they left the house, and the walk through Fleetwood Road took them onto the long stretch of Pauls Avenue. They then headed to the High Street, with the journey taking them approximately twenty minutes. Cramped houses lined the streets either side, with doors opening and shutting as other Indian men dashed out to make their way to work; there was never a dull moment.

The ABC cafe was a small place tightly wedged between a bakery and a fish monger. It was hard to make out how busy it was inside. Steam clouded the two large windows like a sauna. Condensation streamed downwards until it merged to the bottom. Leaving home early, they had intended to arrive ahead of the scheduled time, and therefore showing their punctual nature. However, the person they were meeting was already seated. Recognising the brothers instantly Roy leapt to his feet, greeting them swiftly. Introducing himself with a firm handshake, his height was in full view as his head barely reached to the brother's shoulders. He had thick black hair and bushy eyebrows. His skin was slightly dark, but the most distinct feature was the thick black framed glasses.

These thick lenses amplified his eyes like a vortex, which were blinking furiously. He was well dressed, his long navy coat covering his black suit. Everything about him was prim and proper from first appearance. Extending out his left arm, he pointed towards a small round table near the large window, and then zigzagged through other customers to sit down.

It was a busy place and the smell of cooked breakfast floated around them. Steam bellowed from the kettles on the counter together with the smoke from sizzling bacon on the stove. The condensation inside was getting worse and Inder could barely make out the beautiful Crown Hotel opposite the cafe. He noticed how its size engulfed the entire corner. Gurcharan looked around and noticed they were the only Indians here, therefore avoiding the gaze of onlookers.

Roy had already ordered three cups of tea. Seeing the table occupied, a lady arrived with large white mugs, each with tea stains on the side. Whether this was deliberate they couldn't say for sure, and so just stared at each other, avoiding the lady's gaze.

It was evident the tea hadn't been brewed for long and was of poor taste. Roy moved his mug to one side and started asking more questions. He asked them where in India they were from. How long had they been in England and Slough for that matter? What was their experience of driving? The number of questions were as frequent as the furious blinking of Roy's eyes. At one point Inder asked him to kindly slow down so they could answer each one to his satisfaction.

Just like the phone call their responses, it seemed, filled Roy with confidence. He was no longer hunched forward, but rather his shoulders had dropped as he leant back on his chair. Gurcharan once again touched upon his mechanical engineering background as leverage and employed honesty throughout. They hadn't driven vast distances before, but he assured Roy that between them, they could do it.

From Roy's perspective one thing was clear, the brothers had a strong bond. They were calm and thoughtful, and that was something very crucial to him if he was going to entrust them with his car. Inder and Gurcharan understood why Roy was asking so many questions, but it felt more like an interview than a conversation. They began to wonder whether spending so much time in the car with him was actually a good idea. With a swift movement Roy took out a picture and placed it face down on the table.

Flipping it over he revealed a black and white image of a car. Taking a pause, he proudly informed them the car was a Morris Austin Cambridge Estate. He had purchased it only a few weeks ago and this was their mode of transport. The brothers studied the image of the car carefully. Back in their hometown of Orissa only high-ranking people drove such large cars, and those were Ambassadors. Roy told them the car had a roof rack where additional luggage could be stored. With some hesitation, he then mentioned there would be an additional two passengers travelling with them, his wife and their son.

The lady behind the counter made her way to the empty table to collect the large mugs. Looking at them, she noticed two were still full to the brim while the third was half full, exposing the teabag she forgot to remove.

3 ½ months before the road trip

Evening meals in the house presented an opportunity for all to share thoughts on a wide range of topics. Some spoke of their working day, and of any noteworthy incidents. One of the housemates told of his reluctance to take an Indian packed lunch to work, citing comments of the smell as a reason. The ritual of sitting together was pivotal for everyone.

In India some villages have a council, commonly known as a panchayat. Members are predominantly male and made up of elderly folk who have lived in the village all their lives. Their primary role is to resolve local feuds and provide advice on matters troubling the local people. Mimicking those panchayat style meetings, these evening opportunities allowed oneself to let off steam or seek guidance. Recently, Inder and Gurcharan felt embarrassed that their road trip was dictating conversations.

Chanan Singh saw their predicament differently, and for him this was the growth and development of the brothers. Maybe they weren't just two immigrants living day to day, with a mantra to earn as much money as possible. He'd seen plenty of those types of people, just clinging on to the hope that something will transform their futures. His mind ventured back to the time when Inder had approached him about bringing Gurcharan to England. Chanan Singh was glad he provided that much needed support, and helped the move to take place. It was a small win to mitigate the actions he had taken when he arrived, some he now regretted.

The revelation of additional passengers was a cause for concern for the brothers. Up until this point the road trip was panning out to be three single men on their way to India. But now, with a woman and child accompanying them, some fears had surfaced. Suddenly, they felt an additional responsibility apart from their own. Driving an entire family across unknown terrains whose destiny, and safety lay in their hands made them feel uneasy.

At their last meeting, Gurcharan told Roy of their intention to write to family back home to seek permission. This wasn't just out of respect for their father, but it would allow them to put some thought into what they were embarking on. The words in the letter had to provide assurance, and every word had to count. A phone call would indicate a hint of arrogance, a lack of thought and potential recklessness. Should their father refuse, then the road trip idea was over for them. Under no circumstances would they challenge their father's final decision.

The blank sky blue Airmail paper sat on the edge of the dining table. Unfolding it revealed three equal sections. The horizontal red and dark blue stripes along the edges meant this letter was destined for international waters. At the top of the letter, and carefully centred, were four light grey lines allowing the sender to write the recipients' address. Slightly to the left a label displayed the words *PAR AVION*, **By Air Mail**.

Starting at the top left of the letter, Inder wrote **Respected Papaji and family members.** He then paused momentarily before starting the first paragraph. Thereafter, it was straight to the point.

Ticket prices have not shown any signs of getting cheaper. At this rate we can only purchase one ticket, and I know how much you all want to see us both. As if by God's Grace, an opportunity has presented itself. Someone is looking for two people to drive to India. The car belongs to an established gentleman who lives with his family here in London. The three of them would be travelling with us. The car is new, a fine model from what we have seen in the photo. It is big enough to store lots of food and clothes for us to bring along.

How long the journey will take we are not sure at present but will confirm soon. We understand you will be worried. It is important to obtain your permission for this road trip, and we will respect whatever your decision. But please consider this before you reach that decision. We have a unique opportunity to visit countries that we may never get a chance to see. In each of those countries people live in their customs and dialect, so what a chance to experience this all. Your sons have learnt much since coming to England and we are full of faith that together we can make this journey. This is all we want to say.

Gurcharan read the letter and nodded in approval. He then folded it with the greatest of attention, making sure the edges aligned perfectly. Chanan Singh had purchased a set of stamps from the local Post Office on Wexham Road. The design of the stamps commemorated England's World Cup win in 1966. The heroic achievements of the team were still very much in the public's hearts and minds. After posting the letter, Gurcharan called Roy, and they agreed to speak in two weeks' time. They were confident of a definitive answer from back home. Gurcharan also acknowledged that if Roy found new drivers who were ready to go, then they had to accept their fate.

1963 - The conversation

As evening descended, Inder found his father sitting on the bed reading the local newspaper. This was an ideal moment to have that conversation. Respectively asking for his attention, Inder placed the advert next to his father with hesitancy. Pointing to the words, he told his father England were inviting members of the Commonwealth to come and work. A huge shortage of labour had led to an unprecedented rise in vacancies across different industries.

Without taking a break he continued with excitement, pitching the idea of how much money he could earn. His father remained quiet and raised his head to gaze straight into Inder's eyes. The welling of tears made his eyes shine bright. Then his attention shifted to the doorway. Swarn and Gurcharan stood observing without trying to be noticed, he ushered them in.

As all three of them looked up at their father, he finally broke his silence. An immediate concern was that no one in the family had ever worked outside the city, let alone in another country. Living far away from home, detached from your family was not to be underestimated. Secondly, England was a western country with a different language, and a different way of life. Surjan Singh had no extended family living in England, and therefore no relation to call upon.

Inder dropped his head, acknowledging the direction this conversation was heading in. He couldn't contest the concerns his father had raised. Swarn requested that a decision not be made yet, that their father think about it. This would give her enough time to try and convince him.

A few days later Surjan Singh delivered his verdict on the matter. There was no big announcement or the need for a family meeting. Inder had barely stepped through the door when his father sat him down, and handing him the newspaper containing the advert. He was aware his son had spent two agonising days worrying about the possible outcome.

Rather delay matters it was best to speak his mind. Looking straight at him with a warm smile, he asked Inder about the importance of his appearance. Inder replied with measured confidence. Surjan Singh continued, wanting to know if he would be able to protect himself if this was ever challenged. The reality was in England he would look different amongst thousands of people. There would be onlookers, awkward questions to address, and possibly unwanted comments. Surjan Singh needed the assurance that his son wouldn't strain under this pressure and therefore question his faith. Inder responded in a manner which quashed any concerns that were bubbling to the surface.

His father's blessing was marked with a warning that under no circumstances should Inder ever think about compromising his appearance. For if that day ever arrived then these doors would be closed forever. Before leaving the room, Surjan Singh placed his hand on Inder's shoulder, telling him he also had his sister to thank in all this. It was her persistence that ultimately turned his mind over to allow Inder to go to England.

Getting his father's blessings was an historic moment. However, this was merely the first step in the process. There was the challenge of how this trip would be funded. The stark reality was they didn't have much money. While that concern loomed over his head, Inder would now act on obtaining the voucher.

3 months before the road trip

Over two weeks had passed since their letter home to seek permission. Recently, mornings had started with anticipation but ended with disappointment. Running low on patience, Gurcharan felt now was as good a time to make a call home.

It was a crisp Saturday morning, with dew settled on the grass of squashed houses as they passed. One side of Inder's jacket was weighed down by a plastic bag full of coins in anticipation of a lengthy conversation. No sooner had they reached the telephone box Gurcharan dialled the number, with Inder wedged in beside him. They both listened to the long sound of the dial tone.

Surjan Singh answered the phone. Following what was the briefest of hello's Gurcharan asked whether his father had received the letter about the road trip. ***Yes***, he answered after which he expressed deep concerns, and those of Inder and Gurcharan's siblings. If it meant waiting another year, then so be it. Hearts back home felt empty having not seen them both. ***Save some more, wait longer but we want to see you both*** he told them. He couldn't comprehend what it would be like driving through the different countries but, was mindful the locals may not be as welcoming. What concerned him the most was the potential danger of being anywhere near Pakistan. His sons were two distinct Sikhs holding Indian passports, and relations between Pakistan and India were frail following recent events. Travelling anywhere near those borders would put them all at immediate risk and in the hands of those wanting to make a statement.

Inder and Gurcharan listened attentively, not uttering a word in response. When their father had finished offloading weeks of concern, he respectfully asked his sons for their thoughts. Inder took the phone from Gurcharan and patiently explained that every element of the road trip would be carefully planned. Plenty of help was at hand, and that they would not be travelling alone. With that the brothers had nothing more to say. Their father handed the phone to the other members of the family so they could talk. Before ending the call, he promised they would receive his decision by post.

Three clean mugs full of tea arrived at the round table of the steamy cafe. Inder noticed a warm smile from the lady as she turned to walk back to the serving counter. He felt like the whole world was in a good mood. Maybe word had got around about the recent letter the brothers received from home, the blue one Inder had tucked away in his jacket. A short letter with very few words but carrying such weight, that their father had given his blessing for the road trip.

It was much quieter today, trade at the ABC cafe was often like this for a weekday afternoon. The conversation centred on potential dates for when to start the road trip. Frequently pushing the frame of his thick glasses across the bridge of his nose, Roy was keen to clarify who was responsible for what. The first point of discussion was visas. Roy would arrange for his family while Inder and Gurcharan were responsible for provisioning their own. However, should they require assistance then he would be on hand to help.

He then moved onto the subject of the planning of the road trip, suggesting it be a joint effort. In addition, he would research on suitable accommodation at each destination. There were no promises that a place to stay could be arranged in advance, and so in some instances they would have to find something as and when they arrived in the country. Where Roy saw this as a potential headache, Gurcharan commented this could also be part of a good adventure.

The route was crucial and had to be as efficient as possible to save on any fuel costs. As a starter, Roy pointed the brothers in the direction of speaking to a motoring organisation. Inder and Gurcharan had never heard of the RAC[6] until Roy gave them a brief background. Handing them a piece of paper with the number, he suggested they call the RAC to discuss a probable route. It made sense to Roy that a few options were made available before a final decision was made.

---

[6] Royal Automobile Club – offering breakdown services

Applying a tick against the second line on a small slip, he moved onto point three which read *food*. Traveling together by road presented obvious cost savings but it also meant being creative, and having enough to eat. If they were flying, then the burden of what to eat was not something they had to be concerned about. Once on the plane, you were like a customer in a restaurant high above the clouds, with a guarantee of at least two warm meals and a choice of beverages.

Roy was first to admit he didn't have knowledge of what countries they would pass through. However, whatever country they travelled into would provide an opportunity to savour the local food. But there were no guarantees on taste and so a flexible pallet was needed were they all to take advantage.

Inder suggested that tinned food could be an option. He wasn't keen on it and had never tried it before arriving in England. However, he noticed people relied on it if they were short on time to cook, or just plain lazy. It wasn't ideal but a sensible enough backup plan if they were struggling.

Roy picked up his pen and applied a small tick. The topic of food was agreed and would not need further discussing. Forty-five minutes had passed and there were still two more points on Roy's list. The rumbling noise from stomachs signalled hunger. Raising his hand, Roy attracted the attention of the lady behind the counter.

Picking up the paper-thin menu he carefully scanned the items up and down. Gurcharan noticed Roy focusing hard on the sheet, his nose almost touching the surface. A mumbling sound indicated some indecision, but he finally opted to ordering grilled bacon with potato slices. Handing the menu over to the brothers he asked them to place their orders. Mindful that Roy was paying for all of this, they ordered two pieces of toast each.

Glancing at their mugs the lady noticed they were still half full and probably cold. Gladly offering up fresh teas on the house, the mugs clinked together as she swooped them away from the table. To an outsider this was indeed a kind gesture. But the three of them knew it was a tough tasting tea which was being forced upon them in a show of defiance.

Maybe some of the Britishness had started rubbing off onto the Chhatwal brothers, in that they felt compelled not to decline the kind offer and hurt the lady's feelings. Also, it was only too common in their culture to show gratitude.

While the smell of food consumed the air around them, Roy picked up on the fourth point from what was beginning to feel like a school register. This point centered on how much money they would need to carry. Gurcharan and Inder were none the wiser so Roy explained further.

There was a policy in place called the *Overseas Travel Allowance*, instigated by the Labour government. The policy imposed a maximum limit of £50 per British citizen travelling outside the country. It didn't matter that the brothers held Indian passports; they were not exempt from this rule. Roy pointed out that there would be an opportunity to exchange money along the way however, what type of currency would depend on which countries they travelled through.

Standing up, Roy slipped his hand into his back pocket and took out a wallet. Opening it he revealed a thin plastic card, the same thickness of the napkin resting on their table. Slowly sliding it across the table Inder and Gurcharan read the bold italic letters written across the top, ***Barclaycard***. With a beam in his eyes Roy explained to them that this was a credit card and the first of its kind to be launched here in England. It allowed a person to pay for items without the exchange of physical money. In addition to taking some British currency he was going to be carrying this card as backup only. It was a form of payment that could be used in some European countries, although he was less confident about its purchasing power beyond that.

The concept of paying for something without handing over any money was very new to Inder and Gurcharan. Roy mentioned that to acquire a credit card the person had to be a British citizen with a fixed address. Even then there was no guarantee as the issuing company would need to run background checks to ensure the recipient was financially viable to own one. For now, all this information was lost on the brothers, but they liked the idea of this *magic card*.

To support the *Overseas Tax Allowance*, the government had also imposed a cap on the amount of money that could be taken for fuel, £15 per person. Roy mentioned that it was his responsibility to pay for fuel for the entire trip. Once the route was confirmed, he could then figure out the potential cost based on overall distance.

All the points Roy had on his list had been covered to his satisfaction, but there was still much to be done. Shaking hands with Inder and Gurcharan, he once again reiterated his delight that their family had given permission to drive to India. That part of the journey had been arduous enough, but he hoped for a much smoother ride ahead.

2 ½ months before the road trip

The brothers were under no illusion that this road trip would require a combination of good planning and some luck. At their last meeting Roy had provided them with a contact number for the RAC, but what would they ask? How would they articulate what they were looking for? Gurcharan took the responsibility of making the call. The soft voice of the operator, Brenda, greeted him on the other side. She politely asked the reason for the call. Gurcharan explained he was planning on driving from Slough to India but didn't know the route. Following a brief pause Brenda advised Gurcharan that she would be transferring the call to another person who could better assist.

As the music played Gurcharan turned to Inder and shrugged his shoulders. Then almost instantly the music stopped, and a man's voice appeared on the phone. Introducing himself as Adrian, he replayed back the initial request from Gurcharan for purposes of clarity.

Adrian then progressed with a series of questions so he could provide the right help. ***Have you ever travelled to Europe before?*** Gurcharan's response caught Adrian by surprise. ***You've never driven out of London before?***

Gurcharan went on to explain the series of events that led up to their decision to travel by road. Adrian's tone changed from that of an advisor to a person now really interested in this journey. In the background, sounds of paper being shuffled could be heard. Adrian was jotting down some information as Gurcharan took a pause. A little embarrassed, Gurcharan informed Adrian that this call was being made from a telephone box. He respectively understood, made a note of Gurcharan's home address and said that he would send the information via post at no additional cost.

In his eagerness Gurcharan was going to quiz Adrian on when this information would arrive, but then stopped. Imposing on the advisor would come across as being rude he felt. He'd already done enough in just listening and providing some useful guidance.

Gurcharan was quietly confident that Adrian would stay true to his word. Thanking him for his time and help, he bid Adrian farewell and hung up the receiver.

A knock on the door woke up some of the house mates. A smiling postman handed over a heavy brown envelope which was too large to fit through the small letterbox. The letters *RAC* were stamped across the top. Gurcharan raced downstairs after hearing his name, followed by the comment ***it's something to do with the RAC***. His eyes widened and eyebrows arched further up his forehead upon seeing the post. He couldn't wait to open it up, this was all becoming very real now.

Holding the large brown envelope in his hand, Gurcharan made his way to the back of the house and straight through to the kitchen. Carefully placing it on the small wooden dining table, he started making himself some tea, constantly peering back to look at the envelope. Now settled he opened the top and slid out the contents. There were two thick handbooks and two neatly folded maps. The first handbook read, *R.A.C. Guide and Handbook*.

The second one was called *R.A.C. Continental Handbook*. Flipping the second book around Gurcharan started reading the short blurb on the back. This newly designed handbook included a section on Poland and featured an appendix with information on how to deal with driving to the U.S.S.R (Union of Soviet Socialist Republics or now Russia); two countries Gurcharan had never heard of. The first handbook, according to its blurb, featured a detailed directory of R.A.C. approved hotels and garages in Great Britain and Ireland. Useful if they decided on another road trip sometime in the future.

Turning his attention to the two maps, the Great Britain edition had been marked to show the route from Slough to a place called Dover. Adrian had also marked out the estimated journey time. The second map, a much larger document folded multiple times, featured countries in Europe. A small piece of paper was attached to the map, it had numbers on the far left with names of countries next to it. Carefully placing his finger at the top, Gurcharan started reading the countries in order. As he reached the bottom, there was a short paragraph stating how the map didn't include countries past Turkey, but for reference he had listed them anyway. Adrian had delivered on his promise, and they now had a route.

There was a whole wealth of information contained within these handbooks, but where would Gurcharan start? He thought it best to place the contents back into the envelope and wait until Inder came home from work.

Together they would mull over what they had so generously been sent by Adrian, and it was just the encouragement they needed. Now the realisation had kicked in on what a great opportunity this had transpired to be. But most importantly the good fortune bestowed upon them by God, and blessings from their father.

1963 - The Invite

*It wasn't usual practice for anyone other than Surjan Singh to receive the post. All correspondences were addressed to him, as being the head of the house. However, this morning the postman shouted **Dak**[7] followed by Inder's name, and suddenly there was some excitement. Inside, Inder knew what this letter was about, but remained cautious. He didn't want to portray how overwhelmed he was feeling as there was still a nervousness around the house. Being nonchalant, he asked his sister to go collect the letter. It had been three weeks since Inder's application was submitted and the official look of the envelope signalled this was the response.*

With excitement and trepidation, Inder opened the large envelope, pulled out the yellow paper and unfolded it to reveal the contents. A mixed emotion overcame him at the sight of an official voucher confirming his successful application to work in England. Inder's heart pounded through his chest at the thought that this

---

[7] Dak is a commonly used term in the Indian sub-continent referring to types of communication such as letters, telegrams, interdepartmental notes or fax messages.

was really happening, but at the same time butterflies were floating in his stomach at the thought of being away from his family.

The cocktail of feelings didn't last long as joy gripped his body. This was a fantastic opportunity to work and live in a foreign country. Inder had the chance to earn a good living and try and make inroads for positive improvements. Before he got up off the chair his sister was already at the doorway shouting at the top of her voice. Gurcharan was the first to run up and give Inder a hug, followed by his other brothers. Inder then ran to his father's room, walked towards him and touched his feet. He needed all the blessings he could get.

It didn't take long for the news to travel around the community, with plenty of people wishing Inder all the best on this new adventure. The Chhatwal family had a good friend, Mrs Chopra, who worked in a bank, and upon hearing the news she made it her duty to assist with getting a ticket. She managed to obtain a small discount on the original price, with remaining funds being raised by the family. It had been very hard to pull together the money, with a large part coming from savings each brother had put away. The commitment to fund this trip also came with attached hopes of potential success, and a change in fortunes.

As much as Surjan Singh believed the family had some balance, the crude fact was that they were not financially established. Gurcharan was well aware of the risk everyone was taking to make this happen for Inder, but he had complete faith in his brother. There was however an immediate problem! All their relatives lived here in India, and they didn't know anyone in England. There was no one to consult Inder beforehand, and this was a journey very much into the unknown.

Not a single member of his immediate family or extended had ever travelled to a foreign country. In fact, they didn't know many who worked outside the city. It would have been ideal if Inder could talk to someone, to gain an insight and prepare for this trip. Unknown to Inder, this was a niggling issue which was prying on the mind of his father.

1 month before the road trip

Inder was glad his workplace, and that of Gurcharan's had approved their request for an extended period of leave. Inder's manager had been very supportive ahead of the road trip and they even decided to throw him a farewell party. It was a pleasant gesture, but one that came with an unusual request from his white colleagues. They had never seen an Indian lady dressed in a sari[8], and therefore requested he bring a companion with him dressed in one. This put a young and single Inder in a spot of bother. What was he to do?

He felt obliged not to disappoint his work colleagues, but he'd never been in a relationship with anyone. Inder's house mates failed to offer up any ideas. His only option now was to approach a family

---

[8] A South Indian female garment that consists of a drape varying in different sizes

friend, Mr Suri, and put a proposal to him which potentially risked jeopardising their friendship.

It was a Sunday afternoon and Inder found himself sitting on a small leather sofa in the lounge of his friend's house. Mr Suri's wife, Veena, was busy making tea and preparing some snacks. As the two gentleman exchanged pleasantries, Inder mustered the courage to put forward his predicament. He'd replayed the conversation in his head several times but was still apprehensive on subject.

Mr Suri listened attentively as Inder reeled off the chain of events. His cheeks turned red at the mere mention of bringing along a companion dressed in traditional attire. With hast he accepted the request, without really thinking about it.

Inder paused and looked carefully around the room, he then cleared his throat and continued. He asked Mr Suri whether it was ok to take his wife Veena to the work party. Inder then came to a dead stop, looking down and not daring to make eye contact. Mr Suri remained silent, and then called out to Veena. A sudden rush of panic fell over Inder, now very much regretting the request. Veena entered the room and sat down, while realising Inder was looking very uncomfortable. Mr Suri spoke to his wife in a delicate voice, almost smirking. He requested to Veena that she do Inder the honour of accompanying him to the party dressed in her best sari.

Mr Suri was an educated man who ran a successful business in England, and his wife was the daughter of the famous Panjabi folk singer Parkash Kaur. Both encouraged Inder not to feel bad about his request, as they were only too aware of his humble character, for he was a man of much credit and respectfulness.

Mr Suri parked outside Inder's house, and pressed the horn to signal his arrival. His wife Veena sat patiently in the back. A few minutes later the tall smart looking figure of Inder walked out. Instead of being full of excitement, there was a reluctance, with the thought of asking such a favour still looming on his mind. An eerie silence hung in the air as the three of them drove to Inder's workplace.

Mr Suri joked with Inder to loosen him up. He encouraged him to enjoy the evening and make sure he introduced Veena to all his friends. He praised his wife on her excellent conversational skills, promising that Inder's friends would enjoy hearing about her famous background. If they were fortunate enough, she may even sing a few short stanzas from some of her favourite songs.

It wasn't until they all got out of the car that Inder noticed how smartly dressed Veena was. Her black sari was lined with a thick gold border which looked simple and exquisite at the same time. Mr Suri watched as his wife glided across the car park and towards the party venue. A sudden hush swept across the room as they both walked in which created a momentary awkwardness. Thankfully it didn't last long as Inder's manager welcomed them in. Soon enough the party was in full swing and conversations flowed easily.

Inder's colleagues were exceptionally grateful to Veena for attending the party. She lit up the evening with her exotic singing. Everyone was mesmerised by Veena's style, her eloquence and rich history. Inder noticed the wide-eyed faces on some of the colleagues when they learned of Veena's high level of education and liberal upbringing. While this provided a moment of pride, it also brought along a twinge of disappointment. That there was an assumption of immigrants not being highly educated or possessing the necessary etiquette.

Inder himself was overwhelmed by the show of faith from Mr and Mrs Suri. Back home such an act of friendship would have been frowned upon. However, Inder learned that it was possible to maintain your roots while adopting a liberal approach so as to embrace your surroundings as a step forward.

1963 - A giant leap of faith

There was no need for a wake-up call this morning, and nor was Inder listening out for the sounds of the local animals which would normally signal dawn. Having spent most of the night staring at the walls of his bedroom as way of distraction, he'd barely slept at all. His stomach had been churning all night resulting in a loss of appetite. Even the smells of his favourite breakfast dish, aloo ke prantay (potato stuffed chapatti's) couldn't bring him to eat.

Being pressed by his mother to eat something, he packed what was left into a paper bag for later. His father ushered everyone into the lounge to partake in prayers. All the family remained silent as their mother led the private affair. Blessings were sought for Inder's safe journey to England. His mother's voice remained strong while her heart sank. Inder hugged every member of his family, wearing a smile to mask his emotions. As he stepped out of the house, Inder was greeted by a small crowd. Some of the locals had come out to see him off. People hugged and wished him well for the new adventure. Overwhelmed by this show of love, the barrier finally broke and tears streamed down Inder's cheeks like a waterfall.

The drive to Delhi airport took them via the Holy City of Amritsar, and a chance for a pit stop to offer prayers at Harmandir Sahib (The Golden Temple). Inder was accompanied by Gurcharan, his sister and youngest brother. Leaving his father behind was the hardest part of this journey. He'd given his father the assurance that this was the right course of action, and an opportunity that would benefit them all. Inder's sister had insisted that he write regularly and find a way to call upon landing.

This first leg of the journey to Amritsar took around four hours. It was busy at Harmandir Sahib, with the soft chanting of hymns surrounding the holy complex. Inder offered prayers, took blessings and asked for protection against any obstacles. Sitting cross legged on the cool surface, he absorbed the ambience that vibrated throughout his surroundings.

For a moment, he became still as the calm waters which ran all around the Gurdwara[9]. It amazed him every single time how so many people could sit focused amongst the crowd of people and

---

[9] A Gurdwara is a Sikh Holy place of worship

the chanting. There was such power in this place, and all you had to do was to find that connection. Bowing down and touching his forehead onto the floor one last time, he made his way out. The city was now clogged with traffic.

A further seven-hour drive took Inder to Delhi's International Airport. The flight was scheduled for the evening, but they had arrived early. The roads were so unpredictable and only an expert driver could weave around other cars, tractors and cows. Airport rules stipulated that no family or friends were allowed inside. Hugging his family, the tears streamed down everyone's cheeks. This was the last time in a while that Inder would see them but promised to find a way to contact them as soon as feasible.

Inder didn't have much luggage with him as he'd never been away from home. Carefully navigating through the security checks, he made his way to the departure lounge. As he approached the large windows, he caught a glimpse of the plane which was going to transport him to the foreign land. Overwhelmed by the colossal size, Inder wondered how this lump of metal was able to carry people thousands of miles across vast oceans.

The wait in the departure lounge raced along like a car down a steep hill. Finally, the board signalled departure gate information, and now his nerves were beginning to get the better of him. Inder trudged his way to join the queue of people, his legs feeling like jelly. One by one the passengers walked through the slim tunnel, with Inder politely nodding to one of the flight attendants before being ushered to his seat.

Having figured out that the flashing sign was a reminder to fasten his seat belt, he rocked his head back in anticipation. As the giant lump of metal completed its turn and started gathering pace, the shuddering forced Inder to tightly clinch his armrests. When the plane had reached the right speed, he felt the front elevate, and the plane took off. Inder took a sharp in-take of breath, it wasn't that he was nervous of flying, but now he knew there was no turning back.

1 week before the road trip

Inder and Gurcharan were keen to familiarise themselves with their mode of transport, the Morris Austin Cambridge Estate. Roy agreed this was a good idea and would benefit the drivers.

On-lookers peered from their net curtains as Roy pulled into the street, carefully parking up. Inder instantly opened the door as if he'd been standing there for a while. The garden gate obscured their view, giving only a sneak preview of the car. As the brothers walked to the front, the car's full size glistened in the morning sunlight. This was the car that they would be entrusting their lives with. The photo Roy had shown a few months back didn't do it any justice. It's light shade of green gave a very defining look.

As the brothers stood at the front of the car, they compared the headlights to two drooping eyes. Inder and Gurcharan examined the outside of the car, while looking at each other in amazement. Walking around to the back, Roy opened the boot. It had two doors, one opening upwards and the other downwards, extending the car and making it look even longer. If Inder and Gurcharan had any concerns about luggage space, these were soon quashed. The car's boot was deep and wide, enough for two people to sleep in it if needed.

Making their way to the front both sat inside, taking turns at the driver's wheel. Assessing the leg room and peering into the back, this car oozed quality in every sense. The dashboard was finished in a wood grain effect. Peering out were two round dials, the left one indicating the speed and the right one fuel. The centre console featured a radio with a small clock beneath it. Surrounding the clock was an array of switches which resounded something like the cockpit of an aircraft.

Holding firmly onto the steering wheel with both hands, Inder pushed back on the seat so it made a slight squeaking sound. They both let their minds wander free at the adventure that would unfold in front of them very soon.

There was something the brothers had failed to mention to Roy in their early exchanges. He had never asked them exactly how far the brothers had ever driven. As the three of them shock hands it crossed their minds whether to mention their little episode. However, the words never left their lips.

As Roy drove off, their minds floated back to the incident. Some time ago a friend who worked at the Indian Embassy wanted to go to Birmingham, so he asked Inder and Gurcharan to drive him there. Borrowing a car from a friend, their job was to pick him up from work. It was 2:00am when they reached Central London, but they couldn't locate the pickup point due to not having clear directions. Several hours later, and covering most of London to no avail, they turned back. In the end, they never made it to Birmingham, and that was the total wealth of their driving experience.

But that was all in the past, and a week from now they'd be embarking on a journey they never envisaged 6 months ago. Inder and Gurcharan each put their hands together, looked up at the sky to usher a small prayer and then closed the front door behind them.

Leaving Slough for Dover

It was 7.30am, and the roads around Slough were relatively quiet. Inder drove the car with care, being mindful of his first time behind the wheel. Navigating their way through the high street and across a series of roundabouts they joined the first motorway of many to come, the A4.

A sign reading London Airport brought back memories for both the brothers. It had been a couple of years since they had landed with apprehension and promise in their hearts. That initial period may have been filled with uncertainty, but they got through it. Now they were heading back home to meet their family and share experiences so far.

Roy advised that driving through Hounslow at this hour could head them in the direction of significant traffic. Gurcharan inspected the road map and following his index finger proposed taking the A30 via Staines. Gesturing in Panjabi to Gurcharan, Inder shared his observation that this route would take longer but that they would have to wait and see.

Previously, the brothers had only once ever been to the town of Staines. That visit was to attend a religious Sikh ceremony hosted by a friend in the celebration of a new job. Such traditions resonated from India and were well observed here in England. During this period Sikh's congregated in houses to worship. Here, the Sikh Holy Book, the Guru Granth Sahib Ji would be read to all those in attendance. As they passed Staines, they recalled the warmth that had been shown to them by their host, and the togetherness of the congregation. To complete the ceremony tasty vegetarian food was served and no one went home hungry.

They had been on the road for over an hour, and Staines was now a rear-view memory. Entering the realms of outer London, they headed towards Croydon, it was reaching 9.30am and traffic was blocking the A236. Their car was like a slug crawling slowly along the tarmac. All this time there was an awkward silence in the car, no one was taking the initiative to start a conversation. The brothers wondered how long this silence would last and whether this was a sign of things to come.

Since arriving in England there had often been moments full of awkward silences. Times when they were introduced to co-workers or invited to a gathering where they didn't know anyone. However, where some may have wilted to a corner to hide, the brothers were always first to break the ice. As the car stopped once again, Gurcharan turned around and asked whether it was okay to put the radio on. Maybe some music would help relax the mood and hopefully encourage conversation. With silent nods coming back in his direction, he reached for the dials and searched for a station. Tuning into BBC Radio 1, he slowly turned up the volume to an acceptable listening level. The words *I'm A Believer* by The Monkeys seeped through into the car.

1963 - A different sun and smell

The sound of a trolley swooshing past woke Inder, he was not sure how long he'd been asleep. His long body frame was struggling against the leg room where he was seated. As he re-aligned his thoughts he glanced across to his right and peered out of the small oval shaped window. There below him lay his new destination.

The morning sun, now slowly unveiling the greenery of the land, merged alongside tall buildings and rows of rooftops. Everything looked in order, clean and pleasing on the eye from this distance. He then made out the long grey runway and his heart started beating faster with each decent the plane made. Moments later the rubber tyres clashed with the tarmac and quashed the memories Inder was holding in his mind of family. He now had to remain alert.

Inder Singh Chhatwal set foot on the tarmac of Heathrow Airport in the month of August 1963. He was the tender age of 23 and the first in his family to leave India for a foreign land. There had been fears and concerns amongst family members. But now that was all a distant memory as he patted his jacket to check the wallet was still there. Mrs Chopra, the family friend from the bank had gifted Inder £3 as an auspicious gesture.

Inder surveyed the area around him as he made his way out. The tarmac changed colour and was now a myriad of large square concreate tiles joined together, and it instantly reminded him of the small patch just outside his house in Hoshiarpur. It was very quiet; he recalled the stewardess mentioning it was 4:00am local time. Inder noticed a large building with rows of glass windows, above it he could make out that there was a balcony, possibly where people would stand to watch flights coming in.

To his right was a bright white sign infused with yellow lighting reading Oceanic Terminal. Now inside and heading towards the arrivals section, large black boards ticked showing numerous flight information. Just as he managed to read what was on the board, they would start rolling again. It was like something out of a game show.

Waiting for his luggage to arrive, he was taken aback by the number of white faces around him. People with different coloured hair, clothes and styles. He looked himself up and down, and took a deep breath. A feeling of loneliness was creeping up on him. He remembered the words of his father, ***an alien country.*** *Managing to get assistance in collecting his luggage he was then directed to the exit, but unlike others on his flight, there was no one outside waiting to collect him.*

To Dover and across

Having managed to negotiate an alternative route on the outskirts of Croydon, the car glided gracefully along the B275. It was relatively quiet and that was a blessing in disguise seeing it had been start/stop so far. The break in the radio signal was a sign that they were leaving the vicinity of London and entering new territory. ***Welcome to Kent*** Gurcharan read out aloud.

It had taken three hours of driving before the first break of laughter cut through the silence in the car. A road sign showed the words *Pratts Bottom* and there was a chuckle from the back when it was read aloud. The brothers didn't understand it, but Roy certainly found it amusing. He was about to interject and explain himself when a nudge from Sarita put a stop to that. Realising they needed a break, Roy suggested stopping as soon as feasible to stretch their legs. On his advice Inder pulled over at the next service station in Wrotham Heath.

While Sarita took Kunal to an outdoor toilet, Roy continued to explain the reason for his amusement in the car. ***Silly Bum*** he said as he chuckled while hoping for a better reaction then just a smile. Regardless, Roy was sure many a drivers' who descended upon this town would have had the same reaction as his.

Their ferry was to depart from the port of Dover at 3:00pm, and the long hand on the car's clock signalled a minute past eleven as they left Wrotham Heath to continue along the A20. Soon, the A20 became the A2 as they passed the town of Canterbury; a large sign signalled 20 miles to Dover. Roy was sure that at the current speed it was another forty-five minutes' drive. This meant they were not far off from leaving the shores of England.

London to Kent had taken a while but provided a small sample of what lay ahead. Being able to read the maps provided assurance to the passengers in the back. Gurcharan had taken the time to study the route. In addition, the red markings made by the RAC operator were a great help, and were paying dividends. Very soon the opportunity to experience foreign lands and languages lay in wait with this once-in-a-lifetime adventure, and these maps would help them get there.

Approaching Dover, Inder noticed a queue developing at the port, snaking its way to the Eastern Docks. Looking to his left, the monumental White Cliffs of Dover stood towering over them and a reminder of a lost opportunity for now. Roy had talked about wanting to walk along the cliffs, and to make out France on the horizon. Today this wasn't to be, they had underestimated the journey time.

Inder carefully veered the car into one of the two lanes leading towards the ferry, the *Townsend*. Stewards, neatly dressed in black uniforms with their white flat caps, ushered their car via a hand signal to lead them into the right area to park. This was all very new to the Chhatwal brothers, cars lined up beside them and in front felt like they were aboard a huge floating garage.

Now parked, handbrake up and engine switched off it was time to leave and venture onto the upper main deck. The journey by sea would take around two hours to complete. The upper deck was open air and lined with wooden benches either side. Some benches were already looking busy with passengers. At this point Roy and his family moved to the right-hand side while Inder and Gurcharan walked to the left. Inder appreciated the need to have some separate space, as any free-flowing conversations had been hard to come by so far. Standing at the edge of the railings, the brothers took in the vast sea ahead of them while again appreciating the magnificent White Cliffs of Dover. The air remained crisp but accompanied by a cross wind now picking up pace, their coats providing a warm layer. As the ferry moved across the water, the cliffs became small enough for Inder to hold in the palm of his hands.

The wind picked up again and made the brothers shiver, they couldn't stand out here for too long. Walking to the lower deck and inside the ferry, they noticed the layout of the seats similar to the upper deck. However, these looked much more comfortable and reminded them of the inside of a plane. Sinking into the spacious dark green seats, they closed their eyes and with that the adrenaline from this morning began to settle down.

The voice on the ferry's speaker woke them up, informing all passengers that their destination was within touching distance. Inder and Gurcharan jogged back up to the top deck and noticed Calais on the horizon. From a distance it looked a sea of grey with tall metal crane's lining up the shoreline, the boom of industry calling out to arriving visitors. The brothers wondered if Calais would be like Dover, and have its own castle. The link between Dover and Calais was key for people on both sides even though historically there was little love.

Meeting up with Roy they made their way back to the car with very few words being exchanged. The young boy was now fully awake and chirpy. Firmly settled back into the Austin Cambridge, they watched as the ferry's ramps lowered and the cars starting to manoeuvre onto French soil. Inder and Gurcharan remembered the advice from the RAC that people in

France drove on the right-hand side of the road, or as he put it ***the wrong side***.

Pulling out onto the street, the approaching roundabout displayed a shopping list of directions in a foreign language. Spotting the word *Paris*, they branched off and headed onto a long road. Everyone breathed a sigh of relief while paying gratitude to their respective Gods. The early leg of their journey had been negotiated successfully to date.

Paris here we come

The A15 to Paris was devoid of any road markings, so whether their car was on the right-hand side or in the middle, it made no difference for the time being. Grassy land and wooden shaped pylons lined the road as far as the eye could see. Whenever a car appeared in the opposite direction Inder quickly veered back to the right. The quietness of this long stretch reminded them of a typical countryside lane back in India.

Several miles later, a sign appeared reading *Abbeville*, and this was their first contact with a French community. The road snaked into this small town, lined with its pretty little shops. The cleanliness and cobbly road added a chic flair to the surroundings. What was even more amazing was the number of historical monuments, water fountains and mini roundabouts all wedged into this small space. They had wished to park up and explore this beautiful place but decided to stay on course for Paris. The wonderful

Saint-Vulfran Collegiate Church stood proudly in the background as the passengers departed Abbeville.

They were an hour into their journey and making good progress, passing the city of *Beauvais* and with just thirty miles separating them from the vicinity of Paris. Traffic on the road had begun to pick up so keeping a safe distance was vital. A large van appeared in front of them and kept breaking every few minutes. The erratic behaviour made Inder nervous. A split second later a flying object struck their windscreen, causing a cracking sound vibrating through the car. The speed of the impact took everyone by surprise.

Instantly, Inder's view was hampered and he had to apply a sudden sharp turn onto a hard shoulder. Trusting his instincts and with help from Gurcharan he managed to avoid any collision with other cars. Everyone was shaken by the whole incident however, the brothers kept calm so that they could assess the impact more clearly. With the car now stationary, Gurcharan inspected the windscreen, it was still intact but looked delicate from the collision. He knew that should a small pebble the size of a one Rupee coin accidently make contact then this would surely break the glass.

The thought of smashed glass flying back into the car and endangering them all sent a shiver down Gurcharan's spine. The brothers mulled over what to do next, while Roy remained in the car to console his wife and son. While they could have cursed their luck, they were thankful no one was injured.

It was thirty miles to Paris, and they had no other option but to continue driving. Gurcharan bravely prodded the windscreen just in front of the steering wheel. It was delicate enough that he was able to push out a few chunks of soft glass without disrupting the rest of the windscreen. With holes forged in the shattered windscreen, Inder and Gurcharan swapped and off they continued. Gurcharan drove slowly, peeping through two small holes to see the road ahead.

A soft voice spoke from the back, thanking both the brothers for remaining calm in this whole situation and not panicking. That was the first time Sarita had spoken to the brothers. From what was a frightening experience, the general mood changed. Conversation picked up and the awkwardness disappeared like the fragments of glass. Every so often Gurcharan propped up and down on his seat to see through the shattered glass. The entire windscreen now looked like a jigsaw. Every small chunk had a picture of its own. Heaters were running at full blast to combat the flow of wind that was seeping through the holes.

Those thirty miles felt like forever. It was nothing short of a miracle when they reached Paris with the windscreen intact. It had been a long day and the darkness of the evening had descended upon the city. The lights bellowed from the cafes together with streetlamps doing their best to keep the black of night at bay.

During his research Roy had discovered accommodation in Paris was expensive, and therefore arranged for everyone to stay in a hostel not far from the city centre. The place was relatively cheap and accustomed to having tourists from all around the world. Advance planning ensured they had somewhere to stay soon after arriving in the city. After the events of today, everyone just wanted the safety of their beds.

1963 - Being brave

It was 4.45am when Inder silently stepped outside the airport. The hustle and bustle of India was long forgotten now and replaced with an unfamiliar environment. Although the sun had decided to peak its head out, there was still some patches of darkness and so Inder decided to come back in. He needed time to gather his thoughts and think what his next course of action would be.

Finding a row of seats near the entrance he sat himself down. Several minutes passed in silence, with only a few airport staff to keep him company. Passing time like this was going to be a real struggle and mild sounds of hunger were now echoing from his stomach. Getting up, he walked to a nearby desk, asking the lady where he could get some food. She was polite and delicate, and Inder was able to make out most of the conversation. Recognising that it may prove a challenge to find his way around, she asked a member of staff to take Inder to the adjoining terminal, the Europa Building.

It was much busier inside this part of the airport, and Inder walked along reading the names of the different shops and restaurants. There was the Fortes Snack Bar with its long wooden counter, and low hanging cone shaped lights. Behind the counter were shelves stacked with fresh continental rolls and Danish pastries. Inder didn't understand much of what was on offer so he moved on to the Fortes Buffet Bar, with its bright white counter and shiny black worktop. There were small square tables and chairs dotted around. Inder wondered if he'd be able to squeeze his legs under those tables. Pulling his suitcase along, he ordered a cup of tea and handed over the equivalent of a pound for safe measure. The lady counted it in her hand and gave the rest of the change back to him. He admired her honesty.

Inder slumped into the chair, carefully scanning his surroundings and then blowing over the top of the cup before taking a sip. Instantly, he put the cup down and winced, it wasn't just that the tea was hot, but it had no taste to it at all. It was missing the spices of the country he had left behind, the aroma of those mornings when the animals made strange noises as they roamed the dusty streets. Gripping his luggage tight, he closed his eyes for a while. It seemed this was the only way to pass time until it was lighter outside.

The clunking of teacups woke Inder up, his hand still gripping the luggage. He rubbed his eyes and took a much needed stretch. Hastily making his way from the Europa Building back to Oceanic Terminal, he retraced his steps which took him outside. Inder was amazed how busy the airport had become in just over two hours. This time he walked a little further than before, and everything seemed new to him.

The voices he heard were in foreign dialect, but somehow, he found his way to the designated taxi area. He walked right to the end only to be informed by the driver that he had to go to the front. Joining the queue his mind was filled with excitement as to where his journey would take him next. Inder climbed into the taxi and was instantly lost for words as to what to ask the driver.

The taxi driver was an experienced guy who understood the obvious silence and why Inder was struggling for words. He looked in his mirror for a moment, to see a reaction but, Inder remained quiet. Turning to face him, he nodded his head but still no reaction. The taxi driver knew this passenger had no family here. Better men may have crumbled or broken down but Inder remained astute, somehow hopeful. He certainly hadn't anticipated the loneliness since departing Delhi Airport and was trying hard to keep any emotions at bay. No one had told him what it would be like the moment he set foot in England. But adrenaline kicked in and the desire to survive. Finally, he plucked up the courage and asked the taxi driver where he could go. The driver thought for a while before uttering the word **Slough**.

Inder was one of many Indian men who arrived in London, had jumped into a taxi looking completely bewildered and without a plan. So, he put his future in the hands of a stranger, sat back and prayed it was the right move.

Let's sample some of Paris

Paris was famous for being a chic city however, there was nothing chic about the hostel and its location. The narrow-cobbled road barely had enough room for two cars to pass each other. In the event a car did happen to appear in the opposite direction, then one of them would have had to use part of the pavement to get by.

Three storey houses lined the pathway, with their hostel located at the end of the street. Roy went inside while the others stayed in the car, he wanted to double check their rooms were confirmed. Moments later he popped his head out and gestured with a thumbs up.

There was barely enough room for them all to stand in the lobby area. Roy led the discussions with a feeble attempt to try and pay less then what was agreed. His request however fell on deaf ears. The rooms were not much bigger than the lobby downstairs but, seemed clean at first glance. Inder and Gurcharan's room contained a bunk bed, a small discoloured sink wedged in the corner and an even smaller toilet. Walls were washed with an off-white colour making the room feel as plain as possible. That was pretty much the most exciting thing about this confined space. Such a lifeless room could easily have been mistaken for a prison cell.

No sooner had they slumped onto their beds there was a knock on the door. Roy had been speaking to the owner in the lobby to ascertain details of the nearest garage. He was keen to get the windscreen replaced at the earliest opportunity. Language was a barrier as the owner seemed to struggle with basic English. This was surprising as a hostel like this would have been accustomed to seeing travellers from all around the world.

Roy wasn't getting much joy and his mood changed to that of slight panic. Inder suggested they contact the RAC to help locate a garage, and it also meant whatever they suggested would be reputable.

A couple of Francs later they had a list of three garages. With French speaking skills non-existent, Roy asked the owner Pierre to call the garages on their behalf. The conversation that ensued between Pierre and the garages sounded like someone was gargling. The phrase ***Bonjour avez-vous des pare-brise*** kept being repeated. Only one of the garages could fit the windscreen however, it wasn't in stock and had to be ordered. Foreign cars like the Austin Cambridge were not commonly seen on French roads.

While news that the windscreen could be ordered was positive, the downside was it would take a couple of days to arrive. Roy insisted on the garage coming to the hostel to fit the windscreen, and was happy to pay a little extra. It was too dangerous to drive like this with the added risk of being fined by the local Police.

A strange feeling settled into Gurcharan's stomach and he wasn't hesitant in sharing his thoughts with his brother. First the windscreen incident, now a delay to their journey. He wasn't naive enough to think they wouldn't suffer from a problem along the way however, so soon? The omens weren't great. Inder calmed Gurcharan, reminding him to keep a positive outlook and that all such things were out of their hands and for a greater good.

Now that they were having to stay a few extra days in Paris, Inder and Gurcharan intended on spending at least one of those days sightseeing around the city. Mindful that they were on a tight budget, Pierre recommended a nearby flea market, one of the oldest and largest here in Paris.

The following day, equipped with a local map of the city, Inder and Gurcharan waited patiently for the taxi to arrive. As they sat in the back, the taxi driver turned and looked at them with narrowed eyes. It was obvious he hadn't seen turbaned Sikhs before, and they wondered whether he had come across any Indians at all. After what seemed like a long and awkward pause, the taxi driver proceeded to ask them where they wanted to be dropped off. Not being conversed in the common language, Gurcharan uttered the words ***flea market***.

Hoping the taxi driver would understand the request, his reaction came as a total surprise. At once he turned the other way and ignored them. Gurcharan repeated his request and the taxi driver stated he didn't know where it was. The bemused brothers wondered how it was possible for a taxi driver, in Paris, not to know the location of the flea market.

They were now certain that their appearance, being Indian and not speaking French was the prime reason he didn't want to take them there. ***Parle Francais*** shouted the taxi driver out of frustration, but his actions were unjust.

Inder and Gurcharan weren't about to give up on this situation. They explained to the taxi driver how they were new in this country, had heard many good things about the French, and how helpful they were. Arching his eyes further up, Inder mentioned the road trip and how they were on an adventure. Miraculously this seemed to trigger a change in the behaviour of the driver, who was now nodding. With that, the car zoomed off towards the flea market.

Peering through the window, Paris welcomed them with lush green gardens, fashion shops and museums.

There were numerous coffee shops along the way with outdoor areas to sit. Large brightly coloured carousels acted as a shield against the rays of the sun for the seated customers. They noticed straight away how different Paris was from London. While only venturing into the heart of London on two occasions the coffee shops certainly weren't as appealing as this.

The taxi driver couldn't help but overhear an excited Inder talking about purchasing Chiffon sarees. As best as he could, the taxi driver indicated the flea market was flooded with such fabrics. Finally stopping on a road called *Rue des Rosiers*, they had arrived at *Puces de Saint-Ouen*. Babbling in French with the brothers unable to understand, the driver sped off in his car.

As the taxi disappeared, Inder couldn't help but comment that today they had educated a foreigner. The taxi driver would always remember this day, a day when he met two young turbaned Sikhs. Whatever prejudices he had may have been quashed, and somehow a seed of acceptance planted in his mind which would help future travellers like them.

Sometimes, we can be too trusting

Roy, Sarita and Kunal decided not to accompany Inder and Gurcharan to the flea market, instead opting to visit some local museums. Heading towards the city centre, and hoping to catch a glimpse of the Eiffel Tower, they were marvelled by the elegance and sophistication of Paris. This was a city of fashion, entrenched in style with beautiful stores filled with people and their swagger.

Roy had visited central London a few times, but it was nothing like this place. As they exited the museum and walked around the corner, they could see the Eiffel Tower in its fully glory. The wide cobbled street was the only thing between them and the tall trees that lined either side of this beautiful architecture. The grey steel structure, crude though it looked didn't detract the excitement Roy was feeling.

Sarita and Roy had often talked about monuments such as these and so being here in the moment was a major achievement for them. This was another tick against the list of things to do after an unpredictable start to their lives. Roy was considerably older than Sarita and while this didn't matter to him, others seemed less liberal. They pushed those lingering thoughts to the back of their mind while walking under the large arches propping up the rest of the structure. Kunal buried his head into his mother's stomach, looking up was making him feel uneasy.

Sarita recommended they take a break as Kunal was losing interest, which meant he was hungry. They sat outside a small cafe. A waiter greeted them, and he was well versed in English and took their order with ease. Across the street Roy noticed a trader selling flowers, and every so often he would shout something. His French sounded raw and the waiter told Roy immigrants such as this trader were now commonplace in Paris. There was a hint of disappointment in the way he passed the comment.

After lunch, they happened to walk past one of the traders who tried his best to lure Roy into buying some flowers for Sarita. A native French trader may have backed off after being turned down, but these vendors were overwhelming in their approach to make a sale. However, Roy remained astute and waved away the street trader while trying not to offend him.

Puces de Saint-Ouen, one of the oldest flea markets in Paris was a very popular place bustling with tourists. Inder and Gurcharan were astonished by the sheer volume of people occupying the main street. Stalls and shops lined the street either side, and once you were in, it was hard to find your way out. There were shops selling mirrors, furniture, antiques, textiles, paintings and freshly cooked food. They had English currency with them, and had planned to exchange it at a nearby bank.

The flea market snaked in many directions, and in each direction all they could see were rows of stalls stacked against each other. There didn't seem to be a bank in sight, and so pondered how they were going to acquire local currency. Not ones to shy away from asking, they approached some of the local traders for advice.

The recommendation was to avoid using a local bank and opt for street sellers who could offer a better rate on their money. It's ***bonne situation*** they told them, getting more Francs then at a bank. This was certainly good advice but, with so many people here they were left baffled at who would come to their aid.

Having no idea what a street seller looked like, the brothers walked aimlessly for a short while. It wasn't long before one did, offering them his deal of the day. In broken English he promised them a higher rate if they decided to trade this instant. Gurcharan revealed two hundred pounds from his pocket. Mumbling something in French, the street seller started backing away, telling them he had to be careful as Police often patrolled the area. Requesting that they stay put, he vanished as quickly as he had appeared.

Inder felt uncomfortable at this strange behaviour and wasn't sure if this man could be trusted. However, from his outlook, and the way he spoke this mysterious man looked genuine enough. They waited around as instructed but remained very dubious of the whole situation. A feeling inside them wanted to leave but a sense of pride and naivety kept them rooted on the spot. The noise in the market got louder as more people piled into the already congested area. Now it was even harder to see the concrete floor. The feeling of being closed in led to loss in navigation, and this was no longer an enjoyable shopping adventure.

Moments later, the street seller returned and showed them the Francs which he kept hidden up his sleeve. Gurcharan inspected the money, counted it, and all seemed ok. In one swift action the street seller exchanged the money and pushed it deep into his jacket pocket. Again, he shouted, ***the Police are here*** and ran off.

Inder and Gurcharan quickly walked away until they found a small shop which had a canopy on the front door. As Gurcharan flicked the top note away he discovered to his horror the next note was blank, and the one after that, and the one after that too. In fact, they were all blank apart from the top and bottom notes.

Overcome by a wave of intense heat it took them a while to understand what had just happened. Their hard-earned money had slipped away through their hands, and the trusting nature of their personalities had cost them dearly. Now they had no money to do any of the shopping they had hoped for, and no opportunity to buy presents for their loved ones back home.

Tears welled up in Inder's eyes as he struggled to look at Gurcharan, who himself was reluctant to even raise his head. Feeling dejected, and with what local currency they had left, Inder signalled for a taxi. Before getting in they both turned in the direction of the flea market. A market whose inhabitants were unaware of the unfortunate incident the brothers had just experienced. Every note the street seller had defrauded them had the smell of their long and hard-working hours.

Hopes of buying souvenirs from some of the countries, as a reminder, were swept away. A deep regret filled the taxi with the driver unaware of the brothers' predicament. But there was no regret on the lesson they had learnt. It was the teachings of their parents that now provided solace to their aching hearts.

Papaji would have said we owed the street seller this money from a past life commented Inder. It was an age-old Indian theory related to karma. Inder and Gurcharan had settled all outstanding debts with the street seller, they were now even.

1963 - Let fate take me

Every aspect of Inder's journey from the moment he left his home to setting foot on English soil seemed surreal to him. Rampant emotions heightened his awareness levels, he had to stay alert and carefully observe his immediate surroundings. The bubble shape taxi he was sitting in reminded him of the Ambassador cars from back home, and those that only people of prominent posts drove or were escorted in.

Sitting tightly on the leather-like large seat, he sprawled out his arms either side to feel the open space. Taxi's back home were small and cramped, and if you happened to find yourself in a 3-wheeler auto rickshaw then you'd have no doors either side. A reckless taxi driver making a sharp turn could spell danger for the occupant in the back.

Every now and then Inder glanced up to the watchful eye of this taxi driver, separated only by a pane of plastic. When he couldn't look anywhere else, Inder focused at the reference plate staring back at him, MO3234. He had no idea what it meant but it kept his mind occupied. The volume of the radio increased ever so slightly. Inder could make out a female voice singing to the tune of what sounded like a guitar and a flute. It was soothing enough however he never asked the driver what she was saying.

It was nearing 8:00am when the taxi reached the perimeters of the semi industrial town of Slough - a town whose bleak appearance was synonymous with John Betjeman's poem —

Come friendly bombs, and fall on Slough

It isn't fit for humans now...

Pulling onto a long road called St Paul's Street, the taxi driver parked up. Facing Inder, he told him that this area had people just like him living here. It was Inder's naivety that he didn't understand what the taxi driver was eluding to. Furthermore, he advised Inder to ask around in some of the shops about a place to stay. Raising his finger, he pointed to a row of shops that were owned by Indian immigrants. However, Inder's attention was diverted when he noticed a group of young Indian men walking the streets. He mustered up the courage and told the taxi driver he was going to ask them.

Inder's breathing became erratic as the Indian men neared the taxi. Leaping out he instantly engaged with the man at the front.

The taxi driver watched on as Inder conversed in a confident manner, and not someone who was in a helpless state. Feeling calm and measured now, Inder explained his dilemma and it immediately resonated with the group. Their exchange was brief. It transpired this group of men had arrived just months before with no money or sense of direction.

The oldest of the group, Chanan Singh Sidhu, empathised with Inder and without hesitation insisted he come back with them to their house. As Inder motioned to pay the driver, Chanan Singh stopped him, insisting he would pick up the cost. A baffled taxi driver took the money, but not before telling Inder how lucky he had been.

As Inder walked alongside Chanan Singh, the sense of vulnerability sunk in as his fate was to be determined by a kind and generous stranger. Yes, he had been fortunate in meeting this group of people but Inder was still alone and unaware of customs in this country, even from his own kind.

Bye Paris, hello Switzerland

The taxi ride back to the hostel couldn't have been more different from a couple of hours ago. An eerie silence loomed in the air, with the driver occasionally glancing in his rear-view mirror at two glum faces. Their shoulders drooped further each time they replayed the incident in their heads, it was like a movie stuck on one scene. Inder rested his hand on Gurcharan's shoulder, and they both made a promise never to fall foul of another situation like that.

Roy, Sarita and Kunal had arrived back at the hostel a few hours later. Inder and Gurcharan had explained what happened at the flea market; Roy didn't seem too fazed by this, and it typified his personality. But he was very quick in re-assuring them that he would happily cover all essential expenses. With such a long journey ahead of them, he would rather avoid any tension.

The following day passed in a haze with nothing much for any of them to do. Newspapers and magazines were in the native language and no good for passing time. The rooms didn't have a television which only made the day drag on even more slowly. The hostel served a mediocre snack for lunch, but it meant a change of scenery. Later that evening, the garage contacted the hostel to confirm the windscreen was in stock and they would fit it in the morning.

With the windscreen replaced, it was time to get back on the road. Pierre had been very helpful over the past few days despite the language barrier. It was *au revoir* to France, their first stepping stone into mainland Europe. A country where far too many disasters came too quickly, but in a way edged the passengers a little closer. A place where something tangible was lost but a little education gained. Once they were all snug in the car, it was off to Switzerland.

The rest of the road from Paris along neighbouring Switzerland went smoothly. Geneva, their first stop was at the very tip of Switzerland. The calm roads enabled the passengers to talk about their experiences in Paris.

Roy had opted to stay quiet about their sightseeing experience the previous day. He felt it would have upset the brothers even more and they would start dwelling on the misfortune once again. But now the mood had changed, and he felt more confident. He spoke of the places they visited and the artisan coffee shop they ate at. Not wanting it to seem like he was the only one who found the day beneficial, he nudged Sarita, who agreed with him. She added that Roy was an admirer of fine arts.

During the early period in England, Inder had jumped between jobs to gain experience before settling his feet. Then working in Ascot, he met a fellow Sikh by the name of Jagthar. Their friendship blossomed from the start; both had a hard-working ethic and shared many common interests.

While Inder's experience in England was progressing well, the same could not be said for Jagthar. He struggled to adjust to life in England. A large part of a successful transition was dependent on support from friends who shared the same accommodation and interests. Unfortunately, his place of residence was merely a house where he ate, slept for the night and left for work the following day.

Inder considered himself very fortunate regarding his own situation. He was lucky to have bumped into Chanan Singh that first day he landed, and how well he had been welcomed into the house. Feeling helpless, he wasn't able to offer his own accommodation as an alternative to Jagthar.

Over the coming months, Jagthar's general demeanour deteriorated and the struggle of the situation began to take its toll. Going back to India was not an option as it would be considered a failure on his part, and so he made the decision to move to a different country. It was a huge risk, seeing his first attempt to settle somewhere new hadn't worked out.

Some of Jagthar's work colleagues had recommended France as an option. However, he'd heard the French weren't too welcoming of the English. They disliked the use of the language, which made him nervous as to how tolerable they would be towards people that looked different from them.

Like so many other immigrants looking to settle in a new country, Jagthar remained patient while he made enquiries. His reward was a recommendation on Switzerland being a more suitable location. Inder was sad at the inevitability of his friend leaving for a new life, again. However, he helped wherever possible to ensure Jagthar was well prepared.

Prior to leaving for the road trip, Inder was keen to meet up with Jagthar. It had been several years, and contact had been limited to the odd letter and phone call. He wasn't sure how his friend was finding Switzerland and whether moving to a new country had improved his fortunes. Nonetheless, travelling through Europe presented an ideal opportunity.

Inder had optimistically agreed a potential date with Jagthar for a meet up. But the delay in Paris meant the risk of a missed opportunity as he had no way of contacting Jagthar while in France. A tinge of disappointment settled in the pit of Inder's stomach as they approached a checkpoint allowing them to pass into Geneva.

A small white stoned hut sat tucked away under long green trees. The gravel beneath the tyres crunched as they came closer. The car halted just before the red and white striped barrier. Two guards at the checkpoint approached the car, and a brief conversation ensued. At no point did they check anyone's visas.

The guards had been inquisitive, but more so about the brothers' turbans and where they originated from. Gurcharan provided some context about their own style being influenced by their father. However, he followed up by telling them that a style was predominately dependent on what part of country you resided in.

Acquiring some handy bits of information about where to eat, the barrier rose slowly and off they went. Gurcharan had read that Switzerland was a clean country with nice smooth roads. If the guards were a fair representation of the people of this country, then that was a good thing.

Inder had noted the name of a shopping centre as the meeting point with Jagthar. The native language was French however they found the Swiss more receptive to speaking English, with words pronounced softly. Not knowing how far away they were from the shopping centre; it was a case of trying their best to find it.

Parking at the roadside Inder rolled down the window to ask a passer-by for help. He indicated they were no more than ten minutes away. Before parting, Inder took the opportunity to ask the gentleman to help him make a phone call from the payphone across the road. Calling out the digits of the phone number the stranger dialled away1.

Inder scanned the nearby street, which was bustling with cars. There were carts too being pulled by horses which reminded him of India. The stranger handed Inder the phone as soon as a dial tone began echoing through the receiver.

The man was kind enough to stay until he was sure a connection had been made. Inder's heart raced as he urged the phone to be picked up on the other end, had he lost the chance to see his old friend again?

An old acquaintance

As the dial tone stopped and seconds of silence followed, Jagthar answered the phone. Suddenly the omens looked pleasing; this was a sign of good fortune. Jagthar was delighted to hear that Inder had successfully made it to Switzerland. The conversation was brief, and it was agreed they'd meet at the shopping centre.

With an hour before meeting up, Gurcharan recommended getting something to eat. The brothers were mindful not to burden Jagthar with the obligation of buying everyone lunch. Traditionally Indian men felt compelled to take it upon themselves to provide for their guests. This was a custom that resonated from back home. Even if the host had very little in their pocket, it would not deter them. On either side of the shopping centre there stood a line of restaurants and small coffee shops, and so they headed to one of the cafe's; this treat was on the brothers.

Geneva was draped in a mixture of modern and traditional architecture. There were so many similarities with what they had seen in Paris. Busy roads were filled with cars of all models, and beautiful lush green gardens surrounding tall monuments. It didn't seem that they had left one country and entered a new one. The only feeling lingering was the exhaustion now settling in. It seemed none of them had enjoyed the beds and so were still suffering from a lack of quality sleep.

Roy understood the kind gesture behind Inder meeting his friend. Their stay in Switzerland was to be brief which is why he kept quiet about any reservations he had. The delay in Paris could have resulted in them zooming through Switzerland, but Inder had made a promise to Jagthar. To him driving through Europe and not visiting his friend would, in his eyes show disrespect.

The shopping centre wasn't busy as they all waited patiently perched on a ceramic podium. As agreed, Inder noticed Jagthar heading towards them, it had been almost two years. Inder remembered his slim build from a couple of years ago but he looked even thinner now. There were noticeable signs of fatigue on his face but Inder tried not to focus on that.

Hugs and introductions were exchanged and that seemed to pump some energy into Jagthar. Roy and his family stood around to witness these two friends exchange tales. Inder was keen to know how Jagthar had been settling in Switzerland. For now, Jagthar ignored any conversations around his own position, but was keen to hear how the other companions in Slough were coping with life and work. Inder calmed any concerns Jagthar had, and then with a sense of pride introduced Gurcharan.

Jagthar noted that in a short space of time, Inder had been able to bring over a blood relation to England. Achieving this while trying to find his own feet deserved another hug from his friend and a bout of congratulations. This meeting wasn't just an opportunity for the two friends to catch up on each other's well-being, but also that Jagthar needed to confide in Inder. He had a special request for him for when he reached India.

As it transpired, fortunes had not changed much since the move. Albeit he held down a stable job, but he couldn't see a future where his standard of living would improve. In comparison to England, Switzerland was more expensive to live in. To make matters worse, his residence was quite small and his relationship with those he was sharing not ideal. He often felt like an outsider to his own kind. For now, he had no option but to bide his time and disregard emotions about feeling sorry for himself.

The fear of losing work kept his feet bolted to the ground and he knew nothing different. Inder was saddened by his friend's plight but also frustrated that he couldn't do anything to help. The fact that Jagthar too had given up hope added more misery to Inder's emotions. Noticing they had attracted the deep attention of the rest of the travelling party, Jagthar changed the direction of the conversation.

He gave a tour of the shopping centre and assisted with the exchange of currencies. The day speedily progressed to late afternoon, and with no intention of staying overnight they had to think about getting back on the road. They said their goodbyes, with Inder and Jagthar hugging each other tightly, a tear sat on the tip of Jagthar's eyes as he pulled himself away. They wished each other good luck and soon everyone was buckled in and back on the road, heading towards the West German border.

If France had been chaotic, Switzerland was the opposite. It was uneventful for all the right reasons but presented a key moment for Jagthar and Inder. Although there had been minimal contact with the local inhabitants, their parting memory was of a place where people were very much warm and welcoming.

1963 - New faces and places

Walking just ahead of the group and alongside Chanan Singh, Inder immediately noticed the calm on the streets. Back home, no sooner would the sun have opened its eyes that chaos would have descended everywhere. Today there were no cows pulling carts, no men riding clapped-out rusty rickshaws, and no street vendors shouting at the top of their voices. But their absence was a memory he held tightly.

Turning into a small street Inder read the sign Fleetwood Road. This is where Chanan Singh lived and this was to be his new home. He noticed the houses tightly wedged together and identical. What struck him straight away was how small they were. Whatever preconceptions Inder had about houses in England being big were soon dashed. The front area of the house was paved with square slabs, and some were cracked showing signs of neglect.

In between the cracks weeds pushed out, some as tall as a couple of inches. The brown wooden front door was showing signs of rotting near the bottom, now this was a little like home. As

Chanan Singh turned the key he gave the door a gentle nudge to open it.

Once inside, the first thing Inder noticed was the dark green stained floral carpet in the hallway, showing evidence of overuse. It was a narrow hallway with stairs leading to the first floor. A musky odour filled the air. Inder was certain a mixture of sweat and perfume was to blame for the smell.

A tight feeling washed over him as if the walls were suddenly caving in. The house was small inside and he wondered how the residents must have crammed themselves in. Chanan Singh noticed the hesitancy in Inder, and was quick to calm his fears. **Sleeping arrangements are across two floors** *he told him. This was no different to how things were back home. It was all too common for the men to sleep on the roof top during those summer months while the women slept downstairs.*

While the other Indian men disappeared upstairs, Chanan Singh led Inder through the first door on the right and into a small living room. The room housed a well-used sofa with two mattresses leaning against one of the walls. Clearly this room was a make-shift bedroom for the men looking to get some rest in the evening. It seemed there was very little space to get any privacy.

While Chanan Singh left to make some tea, Inder once again surveyed the room he was sitting in. He'd never seen floral wallpaper before and as he ran his hand against it, he could feel the bumpy, velvety texture. Standing up, he peered through the window and onto the street beyond him. Leaning forward against the sofa, he looked left and then right, noticing the silence outside.

On hearing footsteps, Inder quickly sat back down again. Chanan Singh reappeared with a hot cup of tea and a small plate of biscuits piled on top of each other. Even though he was tired from a night shift at the local factory, Chanan Singh persisted on asking Inder about his journey. As Inder spoke about where he came from and his family, he slowly began to feel at ease.

There was an instant connection between the two, and Chanan Singh encouraged the conversation. Having gone through this exact journey himself he knew it would help Inder with any initial shock he may be experiencing with his new surroundings.

While Chanan Singh spoke about himself, Inder's mind briefly floated to back home. Just 48hrs ago, he was spending his final evening with family in his hometown of Hoshiarpur. That evening, everyone had gathered to give him a good send-off; there was excitement and trepidation in the air.

He could still hear the sound of their laughter and feel the warmth of their love. The air was hot and sticky which made the evening even the more unsettling for him. The music bellowed to the dancing feet for several hours before dinner brought it to an end. As the family ate together a strange silence hung in the air, only to be broken by the odd compliment on the flavour of the food.

The evening drew to a close and Inder remembered the blessings bestowed upon him from everyone before they left. He missed them terribly. On the eve of his trip, Inder had stayed awake most of night. He couldn't sleep and so stared up at the walls he knew so well, for so many years.

The faint voice of Chanan Singh snapped Inder from his trance. He was shown to a room on the first floor, who he would share with two other men. After lunch he unpacked his suitcase into a slender cupboard, while placing his turbans at the top. Inder rested for most of the day while managing to doze off in-between.

As evening descended, the sound of other house mates coming from work jogged him from his slumber. Everyone had been very welcoming to Inder, however he kept conversations at a minimum while climatising to new surroundings. They all sat together for dinner and Inder continued to listen attentively. Trying to follow the dialect was proving a challenge for Inder. While the language was Panjabi, the pronunciation was coarse and slang in nature. On top of that jet lag gripped Inder's body and he struggled to keep his eyes open. That was the signal for him to take leave for the evening.

Lying in bed, Inder tried to take stock of all the events of the day. His mind once again flew back to his home city. He could see himself floating above the houses, all different shapes, some large, some small. There were some with verandas, or open roofs exposing multi-coloured tiled floors. Some houses had small animal patches outdoors, with cows swinging their tails from left to right. Other houses were so old that they suffered from serious decay, with walls peeling away and discolour creeping up like a dark shadow. But they had history within them and stories from many generations. Just like the night before, he stayed awake. But now these walls were very alien to him, and he didn't know their history. He had no idea what tomorrow would bring.

West Germany and camping

The drive through Switzerland was no mean feat but passing through Bern and Zurich provided beautiful scenery along the small winding roads. Avoiding inner streets and towns meant not getting caught in any traffic. They would be driving through the night and therefore stopped at a local petrol station on the outskirts of Zurich for a short break.

Roy took Kunal inside for a toilet break while Sarita took a stroll near the back of the station. In the impending darkness of the sky she could make out the hills in the background. Sarita had remained relatively quiet throughout the journey and the brothers never pushed for dialogue. If she'd happen to join in a conversation by chance then that was fine, but it never happened so far. Inder could sense there was something on her mind, but he kept this to himself.

The three of them waited in the car as Roy and Kunal made their way back. Roy had been engaged in conversation with the man at the cash till. On settling himself back in, a smile beamed across his face as he revealed the nature of his conversation. The man behind the counter had commented on the car, and in response Roy proudly indicated the purchase was one of the greatest achievements of his life. The brothers shared in Roy's moment of joy, but Sarita looked blank on the other hand. Swiftly changing the subject, Roy also confirmed the route onwards and pleased they were on the right track.

While the passengers in the back slept soundly, the sky soon descended into total darkness, with the car's bright lights beaming to show up the upcoming tarmac. The brothers had remained quiet throughout with only snippets of conversation. Driving through the night required extra attention on the road.

Swapping over every so often they edged closer to the border of West Germany. If Inder was driving, Gurcharan would try and catch some sleep, then it would be Inder's turn. Catching a power nap helped freshen the mind and body to maintain focus. Darkness turned to light with the sun peeping its head over the horizon. They'd had their first experience of driving through the night, and it wasn't easy.

The sign for Konstanz was accompanied with the words *border crossing* underneath. A few miles later they approached a large wooden hut with its pointy slate roof, and the checkpoint had arrived. Despite it being early morning there were two long queues of cars in front of them. It was busy and as the car came to a halt, they spotted a uniformed officer with his short cap proceeding with the checks.

The red and white barrier stood tall behind him, and behind that towering trees lined the landscape. Gurcharan and Inder were no experts in cars but they instantly recognised the long round shaped vehicle to their right, with the bonnet proudly wearing a 3-pointed star. The Mercedes car was almost as long as the Austin but had a towering presence of its own. Light cream with a chrome trim working its way around, it was gleaming in the morning sunlight. Their car needed a wash but looked even more filthy against the shiny Mercedes. They only hoped the man sitting in that car didn't look to his left at any moment, as they would feel a twinge of embarrassment.

As their car approached the checkpoint, Gurcharan lowered his window and handed over the relevant paperwork. The whole process was rather pedestrian, but Gurcharan didn't mind as long as it passed without any problems. The wait was always agonising as they never could remember the rules and regulations of each country. Gurcharan quizzed the officer regarding cheap accommodation in Munich. The brothers were still suffering from the losses experienced in Paris. Taking his time, the officer suggested a camp site. He then followed up by telling them about a few camp sites which allowed onsite parking and use of whatever facilities were available, for only a small fee. After a long drive through the night Gurcharan and Inder were pleased to have exited the checkpoint without any issues.

The drive from Konstanz to Munich along the Autobahn took a couple of hours to negotiate. Having driven the entire breath of Switzerland without a lengthy break, they were desperate to pitch up as soon as possible. The sloping countryside filled with its forests and greenery had been a welcomed distraction. But now they were facing the challenge of having to navigate their way to a camp site with exhaustion gripping their mind and body.

Gurcharan didn't get the chance to note down all the information as it was being reeled off by the officer at the checkpoint. The cars behind them were losing their patience, beeping horns and making gestures. They had had little option but to speed back onto the road.

Inder's eyes felt heavy and frustration was creeping in of not knowing where he was heading. What didn't help was the varying tunes of snoring coming from the back seat. They were a few miles from Munich when Inder spotted signs for a camp site. A muddy path lined the route to the ground. It was the first camp site they had seen and was nothing more than a large patch of land with a handful of cars and caravans pitched up.

Having located a spot, Inder parked the car and recommended everyone take a brief walk to stretch their legs and refresh their minds. Gurcharan broke out into squats to get the blood flowing, something Kunal found amusing. Sarita offered up some tinned food, the choice being tuna or spam. The drive from Geneva to the outskirts of Munich had been their longest single run to date. The growing pain in their backs and the experience of driving while tired was a small reminder of what lay ahead.

The road trip was by no means a race, nor had Roy stipulated they had to complete the journey within a certain time limit. But the longer they remained on the road, the longer it meant being wedged in the car seat, and with limited room to manoeuvre.

Driving through all these different countries was a great opportunity, but Inder and Gurcharan were only too mindful that extended periods on the road also increased the chances of something going wrong. They were responsible for the welfare of this family, especially the child and had no idea what impact this journey was having on him.

The ice between the passengers begins to break

The tinned food was neither filling nor tasty, but it was a cheap alternative. The majority of campers at the site were German residents, and so Roy took the opportunity to introduce himself and the others. They seemed friendly and not so distracted by the brothers' attire. One of the residents had a multi-coloured rug laid out in front of his caravan, with two small chairs and a table wedged in between. The whole setting resembled a sitting room outdoors.

They were only staying here for a single night, and so decided to leave the camp site and venture into the nearby town on foot. It was at least a two-mile walk, but this hadn't deterred them from the task. The opportunity to work the leg muscles in a different way was much needed. They had already spent a considerable amount of time with their knees in a right-angle position.

In desperation to find a camp site, no one in the car had taken much notice of the name of the town they were staying in. There wasn't much in terms of local shops, with the options being McDonalds or a pizza parlour. By unanimous vote pizza was the preference.

Some of the locals looked on with puzzled faces as they walked through the front door. Once again it was noticeable locals hadn't seen turbaned people in this area. Disregarding the attention, the walk had done them all some good, and even Kunal looked perked up. As they all settled down, Inder and Gurcharan took the opportunity to break the ice with Sarita. Upon asking her what she did for a living, her response remained vague. The brothers were unsure as to whether this was her general demeanour or hesitancy in front of her husband.

They had tried to show some interest and may have felt despondent until Sarita asked them to address her by her first name. Nodding their heads and smiling, there was a feeling some barriers had been removed and this journey was taking shape in a positive way.

As everyone gulped down their pizza's, Roy talked about his passion for British cars. It was hard to imagine he was passionate about anything. But they were left surprised as conversations opened up. Roy and Sarita had moved to England from India over ten years ago. Roy didn't dwell too much into specific detail as he was being watched closely. They had both fallen in love with the British way of life and what it had to offer.

This was also the main reason for purchasing a car which typified their lifestyle and Britishness. Roy hadn't told anyone back home about the car as it was going to be a surprise. Inder and Gurcharan noticed that beaming smile again, he was indeed in love with this car. That thought added a little more pressure to the brothers; the driving had to be even more careful and focused if it wasn't already.

The exhaustion from the past few days was catching up with them all as the conversations dried up once again. But with every small leg of the journey the brothers were getting a little more insight into the passengers they were transporting. The destination was still far off and there was plenty of time to get to know more about each other. The intrigue around Roy and Sarita's background dwelled on the brother's minds. They were still left wondering what the motives might be behind this trip and whether they were like their own.

On leaving the restaurant. they headed back to the camp site. It was much quieter now with only a few inhabitants pitched outside their vehicles. Gurcharan noticed a member of one family taking a long hard gaze at him. But it wasn't a gaze that made him feel uneasy, but more an inquisitive one followed by a nod.

Inder grabbed some blankets from the car and laid them on the slightly damp grass. The weather was surprisingly mild for an October. Kunal sat on his mother's lap and began to fall asleep; it had been all too much for the child. Inder was certain Kunal must have been suffering from boredom by now but was not able to express his feelings. But then the poor boy had no choice. As they took in the quiet surroundings of the open space, two people from another caravan approached them offering some wine.

While the brothers kindly declined, Roy gladly obliged, lifting the plastic cup to his nose to have a smell. Taking a small gulp, he swished it around in his mouth, a behaviour the brothers found most peculiar having never seen this before. He then nodded in approval to his wife who stared back but remained silent. Roy didn't have much to offer in return, but out of courtesy handed over some tins of food.

Sitting on the floor infused a kind of closeness within the group, and this encouraged Sarita to talk a little more about herself. She worked as a teacher for a local school in Slough but had achieved her education in India. She spoke mostly in Hindi however when she did switch to English, it was well spoken, and indeed a sign of a good education. This road trip had resulted in her having to take an extended break from teaching with no concrete plans thereafter.

Roy spoke of his textile business that he'd been running in Slough for just over seven years. In that time, he had established good relationships with other local retailers, and this was providing them with a steady income. After hearing this the brothers were impressed. While they were proud of their own achievements, it was a huge step up to starting your business from nothing. This took bravery and an appetite for risk, something they found most inspiring. It was commendable how Roy and Sarita had managed to work, run a business and start a family in a foreign country. It resonated a success story considering they had no family nearby.

The conversation then switched to Kunal. He had still been attending primary school when they pulled him out. Although personal reasons were cited the school authorities were apprehensive about the parents' decision.

In the few days they had been together, Kunal had largely remained reserved, and never showed any resistance or frustration. Inder and Gurcharan were amazed at the level of calmness and patience the boy had shown, seeing he had spent these days cramped in limited space. There were only so many seating combinations one could try out.

With the evening turning chilly, preparations were made for sleeping. The ground was not comfortable and so everyone clambered back into the car for the night. Thankfully, the Chauhan family were a short bunch, allowing the brothers to push their seats back and stretch out those long legs.

Unlike modern day cars, there was no recliner option on the Austin Cambridge, and so the sleeping angle proved a challenge on most nights. The thick blankets with their floral design kept the mild chill at bay and it wasn't long before the air of the car was filled with a symphony of snoring sounds.

Gurcharan was the first to get up, with sounds of the birds chirping into the car. His eyes may have been shut but his mind was no doubt processing the journey ahead, trying to map out roads and streets. Inder was going to be behind the wheel so he slept in a little longer. Gurcharan made provisions to acquire some hot water for tea. They had brought with them two tin boxes, one bursting with tea bags and the other full to the brim with coffee.

The clunking of tea mugs woke up the rest of the passengers, with a hot tea (and warm milk for Kunal) the perfect tonic in the morning. Thankfully, the camp site had washing facilities, and so they all freshened up before heading back on the road.

The next leg of their journey would take them to Austria. West Germany had merely been an extension of Switzerland for them all. But the tranquil surroundings provided time for talking and knowing more about each other. As they drove through Munich, Roy told them that in some countries the Mercedes car was seen as a luxury item however, here it was just a regular car, even the taxi drivers had them.

Austria the ice capped beauty

Leaving West Germany, they continued along the Autobahn, heading towards their first pit stop, Salzburg. There were four exits leading them to the West side of the city and it was unclear which was the right one to take. Circling the roundabout a few times, they were reluctant to turn off and head in the wrong direction. The sound of beeps from dumfounded drivers resulted in Inder exiting the next turn to follow signs for the airport. The underground tunnel covered the car in darkness for a brief while as they headed to the West suburbs.

Speed limits were more relaxed in West Germany, but in Austria the roads were littered with signs. This was one bit of information that didn't feature on the maps they had, and it didn't take long for these signs to start appearing in quick succession. A large sign in particular warned drivers of the 50km speed limit in built up areas, 130km on motorways and 100km on all other roads.

Inder didn't understand what was meant by *built up areas*. Thankfully, Roy was on hand to explain that this was reference to roads or areas where there tended to be vehicle or people traffic. Inder jokingly commented that this would have meant 90% of India was built up roads, but they also included animals. He went on to say it wasn't uncommon to see cows and donkey's pulling carts. Just that they didn't have the beeping horns. Kunal found this funny and it was the first time they'd heard him laugh since leaving Slough.

The 400 mile plus drive crossing into Austria took them most of the day to negotiate, and their plan was to stay here for a couple of days. The journey was beginning to take its toll on everyone. Slowly a realisation was settling in that this feeling could risk spoiling the novelty of passing through the different countries. Gurcharan recalled the advice of the RAC advisor, that most European countries had a tourist office. ***This is always a good starting point*** he had told them, to avoid getting lost.

Almost an hour had passed since leaving the roundabout and heading towards the airport. Unfortunately, it wasn't clear whether this was the right direction, but they persisted to drive on. An eery silence was making Inder feel uncomfortable, with a rush of heat pinching around his neck. Soon boredom infested the atmosphere in the car, with Kunal now getting agitated. Mindful that a frustrated child could lead to further frustration in his parents, Gurcharan proposed they stop somewhere and ask a passer-by for directions. At the sight of the next bystander, Inder grounded to a halt.

Thankfully for them the stranger spoke very good English in comparison to what they had experienced in West Germany. Unable to give them the information they were looking for, he directed them to the National Bank as he was certain someone there would know.

The National Bank stood off a street called *Wolf-Dietrich-Starbe*. It was a tall building with beautiful architecture of which the brothers had never seen before. Parking up, Gurcharan looked over to the back seat and asked Roy to accompany them inside. With some hesitation they walked to the front door of the building, with Inder sliding his hands on the large pillars to feel the texture of the design. Roy took the lead and walked towards the front desk where he was greeted in a soft voice by a lady with a casual smile.

Explaining their plight, they found her to be very helpful, and she then reeled off the route. The only problem was there were quite a few right and left turns involved which they had to recall from memory. Realising the blank looks on their faces, she took out a headed sheet of paper and proceeded to draw a rough sketch of the route. Satisfied that they understood the drawing, she bid them farewell, but not before glancing a wink in the direction of Gurcharan.

The three of them left the bank but not before a repetition of thanks. Heading to the car with glowing faces, Roy explained to Sarita that the staff member had been helpful enough to draw out the route. Handing it over to Gurcharan, they proceeded across the main bridge sign posted *Staats BrÜcke* and into the busy marketplace of Salzburg.

The drive across the long bridge felt as if they were leaving one city and joining another, giving them a brief reminder of Dover. Somehow, they managed to navigate their way onto *Mozart Place*, named after the famous composer who was much loved in Austria. As indicated on the drawing, a small glass building stood with the sign *tourist office*. Weary minds and heavy eyes evaporated for a moment at the sight of the office and there was hope they could find a place to stay for the evening. This time Roy remained in the car while Inder and Gurcharan headed inside.

The place was brightly lit and modern looking, a stark contrast to the traditional architecture of the National Bank. The space inside was cramped by the number of magazines, books and brochures littered everywhere. A soft mumbling of the brothers was greeted moments later by a well-dressed lady, whose initial gaze fell upon the brothers' turbans. Having established that they could all converse in English, the lady introduced herself as Romana, politely asking them what they were looking for.

As Inder explained the background, she listened tentatively, complimenting them on finding their way here. When asked about the type of accommodation they were looking for, Gurcharan stipulated the preference of a camp site. Planning on staying for a couple of days in Austria it seemed sensible to opt for cheap accommodation. Their immediate requirement was to find something close by for the night as everyone was exhausted and didn't have the energy to drive around the city.

Romana advised them to camp up near a place called *Lehener Park*, in Lehen. It wasn't an official camp site but more a public park and woodland, and it being a single night they could get away with it. A large trailer or caravan may have attracted attention, but a car would hardly raise an eyebrow. Lehener Park was conveniently located in between the tourist office and the city centre, thus giving them an opportunity to find something more suitable for the next few days.

In that short space of time a trust had formed between the three of them standing in the office. Inder and Gurcharan felt comfortable in taking the opportunity to cross-reference the intended route through Austria. Romana suggested they could save time if they drove into *Bischoften*, then *Villach* and onto Yugoslavia. She also jotted down names of some budget accommodation they could stay at as they passed through those places. **Gasthofs** she had repeated, meaning *simple* and *cheap accommodation*. Walking Inder and Gurcharan to the front door she bid them both good luck in her native language and closed the door behind them.

The instructions from Romana couldn't have been any clearer. The route to Lehener Park ensured busy roads were avoided. They were advised to drive alongside *Salzach River*, the 20-minute journey taking them right up alongside the park itself. Any deviation from the suggested route would surely have confused the passengers, and they wanted to avoid stopping to ask for further directions.

Beyond the horizon of a steep hill they noticed the lush green expanse that was Lehen Park. As they got closer to the edge, they noticed a boundary of small trees dotted everywhere, some with branches arching back on themselves and touching the ground. Having parked opposite the park, Gurcharan and Inder stepped out and walked across the road.

They walked towards the river, carefully stepping across the concrete path which was busy with commuters on foot and bikes. Moving closer to the edge of the long mesh fence, they noticed a footbridge allowing access to the other side. Looking along the river they could see several bridges like the one they were standing near. The bridges continued far into the distance until they had to squint their eyes. They were all perfectly lined connecting one side of the path to the other.

Beyond the bridge were multi-coloured houses, and suddenly Inder and Gurcharan were intrigued by their peculiar design. Inder ventured back to the car to see if Roy, Sarita and Kunal would join them for a walk. But Kunal was already sleeping, the still motion of the car was the final trigger. Roy waved Inder on, and he understood they probably wanted some quiet moments alone.

The brothers continued along the path until they reached a footbridge marked *Pionier Stag*. Walking halfway across, they stood staring down at the grey coloured river sitting in still motion. Across the bridge the large multi-coloured houses sat wedged together. One was pink, one a shade of yellow, and one white. Each of them had long windows dotted from top to bottom; they counted about nine on the front of each house. But then their attention was captured by what was beyond the houses. Towering above them all were the beautiful and commanding ice-capped mountains of Austria.

Standing in admiration, it reminded them of back home. Such mountains with stunning views could be found near Hemkunt Sahib Gurdwara in India. This was a Holy place predominantly visited by thousands of Sikhs each year as part of a pilgrimage. In that moment, a shiver ran through them both, and their eyes glistened in the revelation.

Gurcharan agreed that this was a safe place to stay for the night. As it got darker, they would become invisible to the outside world, and that would be the opportune moment to drive further into the park. Inder noticed the large trees and shrubs would be the perfect barrier to any preying eyes.

Gurcharan lightly tapped the car window, awakening Roy and Sarita from their brief nap. Hunger was striking a chord all round, and so they had to find somewhere to eat, which wasn't too expensive. But before heading out, everyone took the time to give the car a well-deserved clean inside and get the blankets ready for when they returned. The blankets were placed on the front and back seats so that the returning occupants could just fall into them without much effort.

The diminishing stock of food in the boot was opening up more space and Kunal insisted on wanting to sleep in the vacant spot. His persistence was wearing heavily on his parents and therefore making no promises, they told him they would see on returning from dinner.

1963 - Finding His Feet

Chanan Singh was a few years older than Inder. A short, stocky Panjabi man who had succumbed to Western pressures which led him to cutting his hair, shaving his beard and regrettably denouncing his traditional Sikh appearance. It was a decision he was never at ease with. But the situation never affected his capacity for generosity he showed to others. It wasn't just from the first moment he met Inder but throughout their time together. Chanan Singh was a humble individual whose selfless attitude towards countrymen in need showed no limits.

However, his punishing work ethic had taken its toll on his once soft features. The pressures and stresses of responsibility could not be hidden from his face. Once thick black hair were now receding fast and slowly turning grey, well before he had hoped. He was not a man to reminisce or take self-pity but driven to succeed whilst helping others along the way.

Realising that it would take Inder some time before he got a job, Chanan Singh insisted he pay nothing towards rent or food. From his own experience he knew Inder would find this early period a struggle. Some new arrivals adopted the change very well, while others found it overwhelming. Chanan Singh was not taking any second guesses on how Inder would cope during the initial stages. Therefore, he wanted to help him make his transition from a Panjabi immigrant to a more integrated individual, as soon as possible.

A week had passed since Inder had arrived, and it didn't take long before one of the house mates took it upon himself to dispel some of his own wisdom. He advised Inder on cutting his hair and shaving off his beard. According to the housemate this action would present more job opportunities and Inder could start earning money sooner. However, such was Inder's personality and belief that he pushed back, remaining adamant that such action was not needed and frankly insulting.

Not wishing to escalate the situation, Inder reminded the housemate of the importance of Sikh heritage. Talking about his own family and their strong beliefs, he hoped a lesson could be learned. Not wanting to sound arrogant, Inder pointed to the fact that their own parents and grandparents had lived through foreign invasions. Yet they still emerged with their appearance intact and did not falter or question their faith. Therefore, how could he think about dismissing all that for the sole purpose of obtaining a job. Truly embarrassed, the housemate apologised to Inder, and wished he was around when Chanan Singh made the decision to change his appearance.

Later that evening, Inder approached Chanan Singh and asked him about that difficult decision he had made. He trusted Chanan Singh in the knowledge that he wouldn't be offended. With head tilted down and in a low voice Chanan Singh recounted that dark period which led him to shun his Sikh appearance. What made him more ashamed was that he didn't have the courage to tell his parents. The pressures of not getting a job and wanting to fit in amounted to him doing something he would never had imagined he was capable of.

When Inder mentioned his own experience with the housemate, Chanan Singh was furious. But he was proud to hear of Inder's response and had confidence in his ability, advising him to remain faithful to his roots. Inder sensed Chanan Singh saw his past in him and by supporting his decision, it brought some peace to himself.

1963 – Faith and patience pay off

If luck had a hand in pushing Inder to the town of Slough, then little did he know his chances of seeking employment were not as grim as initially thought. What Inder didn't know was how the history of Slough, a town synonymous with immigrants was going to help him get his first ever job.

Post the First World War, Slough experienced its first migration of people from areas such as Wales and Scotland. They flocked to find employment at the newly built Trading Estate, then owned by Slough Trading Company Ltd who acquired it from the government in 1920.

Originally the land had been referred to as 'the dump' because of the dilapidated vehicles left rusting from historic government projects. There was little optimism amongst the locals and newspapers whether the Trading Company could make any use of this vast wasteland. A trade paper at that time, 'Motor News', commented **it will be something of a miracle if they succeed in converting Slough into a money earning** *concern*. *The 'Slough Observer' had struck a more positive note. Its article on the new company and its vision for the future, published on 15th May, bore the headline* **The New Slough**.

Any concerns were soon quashed, and the Trading Estate became the biggest business park in Europe. Spread across a colossal 500-acre site along Bath Road, it attracted some of the biggest companies. By 1926, the French car manufacturer Citroën had arrived, followed by the likes of Johnson & Johnson, Gillette, The Mentho-latum Company, and the Hygienic Ice Company but to name a few.

While there was nothing colourful about the town itself, it continued to see rapid expansion with more businesses setting up trade. Fears began to grow amongst employers that they were heading towards a major shortage of workers to fill those jobs. But this wasn't just a Slough problem, it was a national one. Local newspapers around the country began reporting on labour shortages left by the war. In response the country took steps to acquire skills from new Commonwealth countries such as India.

Inder wasn't accustomed to having free time to himself and was keen to find work. Not contributing to household expenses made him feel guilty. He therefore requested that Chanan Singh assist him in finding suitable employment. They spent the next few days visiting the Trading Estate, diligently walking into the various factory offices to find out if there were any vacancies for a draughtsman.

Following several attempts Inder finally secured a night shift job in Maidenhead for a company that made radio cabinets. It was a cause for celebration and a big achievement, and one he couldn't wait to share with those back home.

Over the coming months, Inder worked hard which impressed the management team. With a good education behind him his managers would often ask him to help settle any team disputes with other colleagues of colour. His skill in talking to people contributed to a promotion to night shift manager. Inder was now the happy recipient of a wage paying £8 per week.

Six months had passed in a flash and Inder had a steady income. As he became more accustomed to the working environment and its demands, he began to consolidate his position. Inder was at ease with his colleagues who valued his hard work ethic and his jovial personality. Now more settled, he even took it upon himself to help others find work.

Not of a selfish nature he even put in a good word at his current place of work, guaranteeing that new recruits would work just as hard as him. As time progressed, Inder became a popular and trustworthy figure in his local neighbourhood. The friendships he built with other peers who had a similar journey allowed them to put their trust in him.

Word spread quickly and random faces started showing up at the house, requesting his assistance to help complete forms while disclosing sensitive information in the process. Such a swift transition from a reluctant, shy man into a striving member of the house was pleasing to Chanan Singh. He was glad their chance meeting that morning had in some way helped them both.

Salzburger Nockel, an Austrian delicacy

It was a mild evening when the passengers headed out to find somewhere to eat. Mindful not to venture too far, and in fear of getting lost, Roy brought along a notepad and pen. Rather oddly he made a note of the street name as they headed out from Lehen Park. He continued to do that as they walked further on, his logic being so they could re-trace their steps back to the car.

Walking along a footpath facing the *Salzach River*, Roy was certain it would lead to some restaurants. He was that confident that he'd brought along a small bag of Austrian Shillings.

A leisurely stroll brought them to end of the footpath which was lined with restaurants and cafes. They avoided entering any large places from fear of price, however a smaller restaurant with a glowing sign reading *Cafe Tomaselli* caught their eye. Peering through the window they noticed only a handful of people.

Fewer people meant fewer prying eyes staring back at them.

The creaking sound of the small brown door seemed to spring the large waitress into action. Hastily, she waddled her way past the tables to greet the new customers. With a hand gesture she led them to a round table located in the corner of the restaurant. Those otherwise engaged broke off conversations to scan the new arrivals up and down.

As the waitress uttered words in her softly spoken dialect of German, she received blank looks. ***Sprechen Sie English*** she responded back. Inder was quick to react and nodded as to show he understood her question. This chance response was met with a smile and the waitress proceeded to point to the paper menus carefully piled on the table. One side had the menu in German, and the other in English. This was a relief and hopefully ordering something wasn't going to be as tricky.

The table went quiet as everyone concentrated on what to order. Once again Inder and Gurcharan's thoughts fell upon the youngest companion. Up to now Kunal hadn't proved a handful which was surprising for a child in this situation. He was however under the watchful eye of his mother and this could be partly the reason.

Roy and Sarita hadn't mentioned Kunal's age, or what school he attended in Slough. There wasn't any talk of his interests, any hobbies or what friends he had. It remained a mystery which the brothers were not ready to delve into or progress with the boy's parents.

Gurcharan scanned the restaurant, often catching the glance of an onlooker. But it is wasn't the type of look that made him feel uncomfortable, it was welcoming followed by a warm smile. Roy used the time to deliberate on the new route that had been handed to them by Romana. Inder and Gurcharan had become accustomed to the ritual displayed by Roy when he was deep in thought. There was a rub of the chin, the pursing of lips, narrowing of the eyes followed by persistent nodding for approval. While the primary route remained the same, Romana's suggestions would now save them a few hours En route to Yugoslavia. Roy seemed satisfied with the recommendation.

They waited patiently for the food to arrive, but an awkward silence hung in the air. How much conversation could they stir up having spent the entire day together. The clatter of plates cut through the silence. It was a much-welcomed distraction as the waitress placed food on the table.

Chicken sandwiches, a few bowls of tomato soup and some cheese rolls stared back at them. With a nod and wave of the hand she strutted off to the counter located at the back of the restaurant. When the waitress was out of sight, the hungry recipients descended upon the food like a pack of vultures. Suddenly the silence was filled with the slurping of soup, the tearing of bread and crunching of lettuce.

It didn't take long for the once full plates now empty with just a few breadcrumbs on it. Kunal was still working at the soup, only stopping to observe the waitress balance the empty plates along her arm. They had no intention of ordering anything else as this had satisfied their appetites, and there was no need to spend any more money. The more money they could keep on them the better, especially where a credit card was not an option.

A few moments later the waitress returned and placed a dish in the middle of their table. On it were five cone shaped items, yellow in colour all wedged together. Their very shape reminded Inder of the ice-capped mountains he'd seen near the Salzach River. The waitress explained this was a popular dessert in Salzberg called the *Salzburger Nockel*. She went on to describe the ingredients. The cone shapes were often referred to as **dumplings**, she encouraged them to try it out.

While the adults looked at each other to figure out who had ordered this, Kunal didn't hesitate. The sweet smell was holding his attention for long enough and he proceeded to try one out.

The confusion soon cleared when the waitress mentioned it was free of charge. The restaurant owner had felt generous to offer this dessert at his own expense. He had never seen anyone with a headdress such as the one worn by Gurcharan and Inder. He was quite amazed by it seeing Salzberg was a popular place with many tourists but none like the brothers.

The waitress signalled to the restaurant manager who rushed over to the table. A slender man with pale skin and dark black hair, he pointed to the brothers' turbans while holding up his hands in appreciation. Moments later he left them to enjoy the dessert and headed back to the small wooden counter.

Kunal had already finished one of the dumplings and was ready for another one. He looked up at his mother who then commented to Roy in Hindi that a sugar rush was not a good idea. With bellies filled and polite goodbyes exchanged, the five tourists stepped out of the restaurant and headed onto the footpath, along the riverbank to where they had parked the car.

Lehen Park was quiet now, with just the faint sounds of horns being heard every so often. The streetlights on the edge of the park were a welcome assistance, but not ideal for keeping a low profile. Once everyone was in the car, Gurcharan slowly steered the vehicle further into the park. They carefully veered along the myriad of pathways, heading towards a more central spot.

The pathways were solid concrete, and their car glided along like a fish in a pond, wriggling in a graceful manner. As they ventured deeper, the mystery of what was in front of them only revealed itself once the low-lit headlights fell upon the ground ahead. A large tree with branches curving backwards seemed the ideal place to park. The Austin nestled into the bosom of the bark, with the sound of branches swishing as they connected with the roof rack.

Gurcharan kept the car on for a while as the heaters blasted warm air, gladly aiding the passengers in the back who were now tucked under the thick blanket. For a while both the brothers peered out through the windscreen and towards the high-top buildings across the Salzach River. They were down here hidden away, while the people up there nestled comfortably high within the beautiful landscape.

They wondered whether those people, through their narrow windows while gazing out towards the park could see the silent Austin perched next to the large tree. If they looked hard enough, could they see through the near clean windscreen, and at the brothers' tightly wrapped turbans? If they could see that, would they have been able to see the slight discomfort on the brothers' faces?

Discomfort brought about as they tried to find a suitable head position against the seat. Mindful not to push too hard in case their turbans loosened up.

No sooner had Gurcharan turned off the engine, everyone locked the doors and closed their eyes for a well-deserved rest.

A chance meeting

Kunal was the first to get up, hastily clambering over his parent's heads from the boot, and into the vacant space on the back seat. The barking of a dog was a warning that soon enough the park would be filled with passers-by and joggers. Roy opened the back door to take a stretch. In doing so his short legs nudged Inder's seat, sending him into an alerted gaze in the back mirror. Angling it towards himself, Inder surveyed his beard, ensuring the strands of hair were still neatly in place. He was content no further action was required for now.

It seemed having spent five nights sleeping in the car, their bodies were becoming accustomed to the tight space. How could they tell? The need to stretch their legs was becoming less frequent and surely this was a good sign. Apart from Kunal the rest of them had managed to master the art of having a favourite position.

They'd planned to spend a few hours sightseeing in Salzberg and then head towards the town of Villach. Once there, it would be an overnight stay before heading to Yugoslavia. Not wanting to spend any longer in the park, Gurcharan navigated the car towards the main road. Some onlookers stared in dismay as the Austin crept up the pathway as slowly as possible. No matter how conservative the locals may have seemed, even they would have flinched at the sight of their local park being invaded by a group of strangers in a car.

The city centre was nestled between the Salzach River and the picturesque mountains and not too hard to find. A guidebook that Inder had picked up yesterday referred to this place as *old town*. Along with the book, Romana had kindly given them a disc, which would allow them to park their car around the city for free.

Parking in the area was operated through a system called *Kurzpark Zone*. To park you had to either purchase coupons or acquire these discs, so they were grateful for the generosity shown by Romana. Without such acts of kindness, they wouldn't have been able to accomplish even the smallest tasks.

Today they decided to remain together as it was far safer and there was less chance of anyone being the subject of any wrongdoing by the locals. The memory of Paris was still raw in the minds of Inder and Gurcharan. The city centre was a maze of narrow streets, much like a puzzle but looking all the same. The theme of multi-coloured buildings was ever-present, and they all ventured through an entrance called *Getreidegasse*.

Beautiful archways lined the pavements, further complimenting the city's attention to detailed architecture. A particular restaurant stood out along the narrow street. Featuring double fronted bay windows, its large balcony above was beautifully lined with pink flowers.

Looking up, the brothers noticed people patiently sitting, chatting away, sipping hot drinks and enjoying the food. One thing became evident very quickly, that no one stared at them. There was the odd inquisitive gaze at their turbans, but it was clear people here just minded their own business. It was noticeable how expensive items were in some of the shops. With a limited budget their choices were drastically restricted. Roy was quick to assist with how much something would cost in comparison to England, and much to the annoyance of Sarita.

The narrow street led them to an open market square, and it was as if they had squeezed out of a funnel and into a whole new place. The market square was lined with various stalls and café's hosting small round tables and chairs for extended seating. This was no different to back home in India where tables and chairs were littered outside, especially at those *chai-walla* places.

The vibrancy and culture echoed throughout the marketplace, a stark contrast to Slough. No sooner had they started browsing that they heard someone shout in their direction. Inder turned to Gurcharan asking him if he too heard someone say the word *paaji* (brother). Once again someone shouted in their direction, only this time the sound was much closer and then all of sudden a young Indian man appeared before them.

The young man's delight at seeing the brothers was illustrated in the tight hug he gave them both. Inder and Gurcharan barely had time to study their new friend, but the warmth shown instantly told them this man was of good intentions. Introductions were done, and Roy gestured to Inder that they would leave the three of them to talk.

The conversation took place in Panjabi, although the man's dialect was coarse. He introduced himself as Kulvinder and told them he originated from Phagwara in Panjab. Kulvinder had arrived in Austria only a few years ago with some friends.

He was happy to hear about their road trip, but sad that their stay here was to be brief. As was custom within the Indian culture he insisted that they all come to his house for dinner in the evening. Meeting them today reminded him of home and his family. Not wanting to sound rude, the brothers humbly accepted Kulvinder's invitation however, that it was likely only the two of them would come. They were mindful that Roy and his family tended not to stay out too late due to Kunal.

Kulvinder mentioned that he lived and worked in a town called *Bischofshofen*, and earned his living on the farms owned by a local Austrian family. He told them Bischofshofen was approximately an hour's journey from Salzberg and that there were various types of accommodation at which they could stay for the night. Handing over his address, and looking forward to meeting them in the evening, he headed deep into the market.

Roy and Sarita were comfortable with staying the night in a different town but on the proviso that they left Salzberg soon so they could find suitable accommodation. However, this meant a change of plan, and so driving straight to Yugoslavia the following day.

Gurcharan and Inder had to remind themselves that their prime objective was to reach India safely. Sightseeing was an ideal opportunity but, unplanned time on the road also increased their chances of something going wrong.

Brief, but a taste of home

The A10 autobahn provided the quickest route to Bischofshofen, a town in stark contrast to Salzberg. They left behind the cultural atmosphere of a large city and entered an industrial area entrenched with a history of economic decline and religious warfare.

Straight away it was evident this place was missing the multi-coloured buildings, the double fronted restaurants and poetic cafes of Salzberg. But what it lacked in beauty, it made up in cheap accommodation. Bischofshofen was awash with homes offering rooms for the night, and it didn't take long for them to secure something which included a hearty breakfast the following morning.

If there was something that annoyed the passengers the most, it was the constant loading and unloading of luggage. Untying all the straps, and then having to stand on the door ledge and stretch over. Then there was the dragging into countless hotel lobby's and up multiple stairs.

Camp sites provided some relief as they didn't have to worry too much about lifting luggage around. On those occasions it could be left on the roof rack and only with a blessing would it still be there the next day. Even if someone climbed aboard the roof to help themselves, the passengers would never have noticed as being so drowned out in sleep.

The owners of the house were an elderly couple, and the house itself was small, with dark brick and three bay windows at the front. The ground floor had a living room with a television, a sofa and coffee table. A narrow walkway led to the kitchen at the back where there was a dining table. This would be their morning spot for breakfast.

Upstairs there were two rooms, one was larger than the other and so Roy opted for this one. The brothers dragged their luggage inside and up the stairs. The marks on the walls told them this was a regular spot for tourists. The place looked like it was peeling away, with the owners in no hurry to improve things.

Gurcharan opened the door to find a considerably small and plain looking room. Dusty bed sheets welcomed them, with dark grey walls and a picture depicting a sunflower. The room had two small windows overlooking a neglected garden. Stained white netted voile provided some privacy, and complimented by bright orange and brown striped curtains. It wasn't at all welcoming, but it was very cheap and that was that.

Much to their surprise, Roy had indicated that they would accompany the brothers to Kulvinder's house for evening dinner. Shortly after settling in, Inder made his way to Roy's room to confirm a leaving time. However, as he got closer to the paper-thin door, he could hear loud voices; if he wasn't mistaken it sounded like arguing.

Inder hesitantly knocked on the door, and Roy opened it looking somewhat frustrated but trying to keep his cool. Asking him what time they would be ready to head out, Roy stood there silently for a moment. Then pulling a face, he declined while asking Inder to offer his apologies to Kulvinder. Catching a glimpse of Sarita in the background, Inder didn't probe the situation much. It now remained a matter of how they would get to Kulvinder's house.

Inder stood at the same spot for a moment and then knocked on the door again. This time there was a delay before Roy opened it. The look on his face signalled a plea for help but Inder couldn't keep Roy at the door forever. Soon enough he would be plunged back into whatever deep discussions were taking place behind the closed door.

Without thinking, Inder asked whether they could borrow the car for the evening. In a swift movement Roy nodded in approval and handed over the keys. Inder dashed back to his room just in case Roy changed his mind. Obviously, he was too distracted at this point to worry about leaving his beloved car with the brothers.

Having navigated their way to Kulvinder's house with help along the way, they found his flat on a congested side street. It resembled a busy colony in Delhi, all stuck together with narrow windows peering out.

Along this journey they were realising that the world outside of their homeland was no different. It wasn't all like what the magazines had shown during one of their trips to a travel agent in Slough. The glossy pictures showing clean roads, lush green forests and fields with mountainous backdrops. This was all true but there was another reality, one of immigration and daily struggles of people tucked away from the beauty.

They felt hesitant about leaving the Austin Cambridge parked on the side road. The boot was full of tinned food which they hadn't moved out. The car shone like a beacon on the street, but it was a risk they had to take. As soon as they approached the front door, the strong fragrance of traditional Indian cooking flowed through the open front windows.

The smell was all too familiar, and it reminded them of home. In that moment they were back standing in front of the stove as their mother swirled the large wooden spoon in clockwise motion to maintain the consistency. Saag and makki de roti[10] had a distinct smell, and it only got stronger as Kulvinder opened the door to welcome the brothers in.

The space in the flat was very tight. In comparison, their house in England was much larger and allowed for better freedom of movement. Once again, they counted their lucky stars for the generosity shown by Chanan Singh a few years back.

Moving through the narrow corridor, they went into the lounge area and were greeted by several other men. They all lived together, which made the brothers wonder just how they all managed in such a confined space. The crackling of pakoras and samosas could be heard in the kitchen next door. Their hosts had made

---

[10] Popular vegetarian dish from the Panjab region consisting of Saag (made from mustard seeds and spinach) and makki de roti (made from unleavened cornbread) – renowned for its tasteful combination.

every effort in preparing and presenting Inder and Gurcharan with a variety of traditional dishes.

All the food showcased culinary skills of these men. They had equipped themselves with the single most important skill, the ability to cook. Like Gurcharan and Inder, they too had no relatives in Austria, with no one able to educate them on customs of a new country. But that they could cook so well gave them a small sense of independence.

The taste of the food was authentic and at the very first bite Gurcharan and Inder blew out a huge sigh. Worried if the food was too spicy, the brothers were quick to quash any fears, stating their reaction was in total joy. Having been on the road for so many days, they had lived on bland food and craved for a taste closer to home.

The evening flowed with good food and exchange of stories about the struggles and successes of moving to a foreign land. Kulvinder had come to Germany in the hope of settling on a permanent basis but it didn't go to plan. There was more resistance to non-German people obtaining work then he had anticipated. Based on advice from a close friend Austria offered a better opportunity and so he moved in with new friends.

With very little education Kulvinder experienced an immediate struggle but this didn't deter him, and together with his new friends made a good fight of the situation. The farms he explained were hard work with long hours, always having to be crouched in one position picking fruit and vegetables.

The sad irony was that back home these men were the masters of their own farmlands. Acres of nourished land stretching as far as the eye could see but here, they were governed by masters of another kind. If there had been a sense of pride in them, it had soon evaporated in the quest of integrating into a new community and finding their feet.

The brothers listened attentively to the stories and experiences of their hosts. The transition into Austrian life had been tough on them all. But the key to their survival wasn't just that they were all crammed together in this small flat, or that they spent almost the whole day together on the farms, but it was to do with the traditional Indian food.

A majority of all their meals were freshly cooked from scratch. Collectively working in the small kitchen, cutting vegetables, preparing the base sauce, eating together and washing up presented a mighty effort but some relief. It was also an opportunity for them all to engage in dialog, to share any problems and listen to solutions. Loneliness would drive a person insane and so they had all promised a duty of care towards each other. With little money left over after expenses the chance of eating out was not a reality. Just like Inder and Gurcharan, these housemates also sent a large portion of what they earned back home.

Without noticing, time had flown by quickly and it was now very late. On the advice of Kulvinder, it was decided that the brothers spend the night with them and drive off in the morning. There was some resistance from the brothers as they didn't want to burden their hosts, but their plea fell on deaf ears. Most of the night was spent playing a traditional card game of rummy to the point that their eyes couldn't remain open anymore.

Before sleeping, Inder pondered about Roy. Would he be peering out of the house window right now, panicking that the brothers hadn't yet arrived? He could imagine Roy making several pit stops to their room, and standing there wrestling with his thoughts. Gurcharan calmed his brothers fears, telling him that in reality Roy was probably asleep, avoiding the gaze of Sarita.

The following morning the house was busy with activity, as some of the housemates got ready to start their shift at the farms. As if Kulvinder hadn't been so generous already, he decided to take the day off. Instead he wanted to take the brothers to a local festival. In doing so, he had sacrificed a day's pay and the brothers knew the value of what he had done.

Kulvinder sat in the front seat, and he was amazed that this car had been their transport and home for the past week. They decided to stop by and ask Roy and his family to come along. As the car pulled up, an apprehensive Gurcharan made his way inside. He was now nervous about what Roy's reaction would be. But to his surprise, Roy didn't even mention about their whereabouts last night. He had complete trust in them both and this was a major achievement on the part of the brothers.

Getting everyone in was a tight squeeze, with four wedged together in the back. Inder was driving and Sarita joined him at the front; it was not lady like to sit wedged at the back with another man who she didn't know. Glancing across, Inder noticed Sarita wearing a smirk across her face, the front seat it seemed was a place of liberation. Maybe she had given up all hope of ever sitting at the front during the road trip, to be allowed some freedom and see the road in all its glory. Rolling down the window she waved her hand outside to feel the rush of the wind. The reaction was like that of a child who had finally got the toy it wanted.

The local festival featured an array of food stalls representing parts of Europe and India. It was a pleasant surprise to see this cultural mix in a small town like this. Roy and Sarita took Kunal to the rides and they all decided to meet at an agreed time near the entrance. Inder and Gurcharan repaid Kulvinder's hospitality by treating him to lunch and buying him an ornament for the flat. They purchased some coats for themselves, mindful the climate ahead may not be as pleasant as in Europe, and the price was a fair one too.

It proved to be another memorable day. Kulvinder was dropped off at his flat, hugs were exchanged with an appreciation of what this chance meeting had led to. Inder and Gurcharan would never forget the hospitality and generosity shown by Kulvinder and his friends. This was true Panjabi custom, in cancelling your own plans for someone who you didn't really know and making their stay as comfortable as possible.

There would be no further respite today, with the challenge ahead being a long drive towards Yugoslavia. They clearly recalled the advice from the assistant at the RAC, that the luxury of smooth roads may well come to an end at this point.

1964 - Integration underway

It had been seven months since Inder arrived in England and every effort was made within the house to make him feel at ease. His housemates were predominately of Jatt caste (heritage of landowners), whereas he was of Katri caste (entrepreneurs). Although Inder was not a strong believer in the caste system, he was certainly becoming well acquainted with the dialect of those of Jatt origin.

One of the most notable things was the need to attach the term 'daal' after every food dish. Daal is reference to a lentil-based dish and consumed as part of a vegetarian diet. Therefore, it sounded very peculiar to Inder when he heard phrases like "Kokri De Daal" (chicken-based lentil dish) or "Gosht De Daal" (lamb-based lentil dish), when in fact lentils didn't even feature as an ingredient.

Trying not to offend anyone, Inder went along with this for a while but his curiosity got the better of him eventually. Bringing up the topic over dinner one evening, it transpired that the term daal was used to describe any dish which was runny in texture. This was all a new learning curve for him.

It was a Saturday morning and in a long time Inder was not working overtime. He decided to venture into Slough High Street to explore the town a little more. He was now quite accustomed to the route which took him along Fleetwood road, and then onto St Pauls Avenue. Here he would cover the entire length of the street, with another left turn onto Stoke Road which would eventually join up onto the High Street.

It was the first time he had visited the High Street on his own, but he was confident that if nothing else, this would be an adventure. The High Street was a busy affair on any given day and even more so on a Saturday as it coped with a sea of shoppers. While there was no vibrancy about the town centre, the fashion came in all guises.

Young ladies wore matching jackets and skirts with high heel shoes, and hair neatly tucked away. Older ladies were snuggly wrapped in long overcoats, with some wearing thin headscarves to keep their hair tidy. The men wore suits with tight knotted ties, they all looked very business-like and important.

Cars and cycles equally shared the road; Inder was amazed to see the number of women riding cycles, unheard of back home. Above him, strings could be seen tied between lamp posts with small flags hanging off them depicting the Union Jack. This was prevalent everywhere and showed Slough as a proud and patriotic town.

Not many immigrants frequented the High Street as weekends meant overtime opportunities to earn more money. This wasn't a bad thing and Inder had nothing against any of his fellow countrymen trying to turn every spare moment into a working opportunity. He just wished there were more faces like his scattered around the local town so that he wouldn't feel out of place.

Walking along the pavement, he carefully observed the names of the stores he passed, storing their visual shop front in his mind. There was the Suters Department store with its carefully styled windows showcasing premium products, ranging from clothing to electrical items. The large windows were carefully protected from the rays of the sun by draping striped awnings.

Squeezed in between the next department store was a small card and wrapping shop. Inder noticed its windows beautifully lined with colourful wrapping paper and matching greeting cards. There were cards for birthdays, weddings, engagements, for brothers, sisters, mothers and fathers. Inder had never seen such an array of greeting cards, suited for every family relative.

As he scanned further down the shelf, he noticed cards for sad occasions, for wishing someone well, for moving home and even for a new job. There was something for every occasion, and it provided a further insight into the nature of British people and their buying habits.

Moving on, he picked up on the smell of food coming from the direction in which he was headed. As the smell grew stronger, his stomach started churning with hunger. Inder arrived in front of a small shop with misty windows, the sign above reading Horseshoe Cafe. At first, he was hesitant about going in, gripping the door handle and contemplating his next move.

Here he was, on his own having never really ventured out. Then suddenly his hand slipped from the handle as someone on the other side pulled the door. **Excuse me mate** *came the words as Inder moved to one side, there was no turning back now as he was left exposed to the people sitting inside. Stepping in, the sound of chatter was suddenly replaced with a hush. Inder looked downwards as a sea of blank faces locked eyes on him, like he had just landed from another planet.*

The awkward silence gave Inder an uneasy feeling. His legs felt heavy and he was momentarily unable to move in any direction. The cafe wasn't very big, but it felt even smaller now and he was almost touching the table next to him. A large man in a stripy jumper sat at the table breathing heavily as he cut the food on his plate. Inder finally lifted his head, and the lady behind the counter walked towards him. **Sit over there and I'll be with you in a bit my luv.** *He was taken aback by the over friendliness of the lady who called him luv. Had she instantly fallen for him he thought?*

There was a menu on the table with writing on both sides. Inder picked it up and started reading it, soon realising why the other housemates were so reluctant to venture out on their own. There were items he had never heard of, and so how was he supposed to order anything? Scanning down, he had the choice of bacon, tomatoes, streaky bacon, scrambled eggs, grilled bacon and sliced potatoes, porridge, anchovy toast, kippers, toast and butter, bubble and squeak, a full English, boiled eggs, side of beans, grilled mushrooms, sausage in a bap and fish cakes.

Inder had to scan the menu a few times over to see if there was anything that sounded familiar or something he could visualise.

Egg was the only item that he seemed confident with so asked for it boiled with a cup of tea.

When it arrived, the egg was bland but cooked, which Inder polished off quickly. He then sat for a short while enjoying his tea. Pleased that he had mustered up the courage to come out to the cafe, Inder felt a sense of pride that he'd managed to order something without any assistance. It was a big step for him and would be a great source of discussion in the evening with the other housemates. Walking out and retracing the route back to the house, there was a small spring in his step.

1964 – Something else is brewing

Gurcharan missed Inder, but the letters kept their bond firmly in place. Luckily, his job kept his mind off the separation he was feeling. It was the start of the month which meant several contractors visiting the steel plant where he worked. This was an on-going arrangement for these contractors to stop over for a couple of days to offer their expertise and discuss progress.

For Gurcharan, it meant a visit from Mr Nanda with whom he had formed a good relationship. Like before, Mr Nanda would be accompanied by his family, some of whom would take the opportunity to see the plant. During his last visit, which was unplanned, Mr Nanda had asked Gurcharan to give his family members an insight into some of the jobs he performed. It was during that brief insight that a particular member of the family struck a chord with him.

As lunchtime loomed Gurcharan knocked on the office door. Walking in, his eyes instantly scanned the room to where Mr Nanda's daughter was sitting patiently. Pleased to see him after such a long time, Gurcharan offered to take them both for lunch.

Mr Nanda declined but requested that his daughter Charanjit continue without him.

The walk from the office to the small restaurant just outside the steel plant was short but the silence seemed a lifetime. A cup of tea and some snacks were ordered, Gurcharan finally plucking up the courage to speak, and asking Charanjit what she did back in her hometown. Mesmerised by every word travelling through his ears and into his mind, this opportune meeting developed sensations he could not describe. It felt like he was trapped in some romantic Bollywood movie. Classic love songs were replaying in his mind and the butterflies in his stomach were dancing to every tune.

The brief time they had spent in each other's company seemed to have had a profound effect on them both and mutual feelings had begun to grow stronger.

Their confidence in each other blossomed to the point that six months later Gurcharan took the first step in informing his family of his feelings for Charanjit. He humbly requested his father speak to Mr Nanda about this. Gurcharan had assumed that Mr Nanda would take gladly to this request. All that remained now was for his family to start the big conversation.

It gets rocky in Yugoslavia

Europe offered the pleasure of smooth roads and open motorways. With arms wide open, it gave the Austin Cambridge the road it deserved, mile after mile, without asking anything in return.

The drive from Bischofshofen to the borders of Yugoslavia via Graz took several hours to negotiate. The fading light meant no time to stop over for a break. Rough roads would now test the car and its passengers' nerve and resilience.

Sleeping soundly in the back, Roy, Sarita and Kunal were awoken by the crunching sound of the surface. Peering either side of the car, the grey tarmac had now transformed into a beige sea of stones and small rocks. Gurcharan, with hands gripped tightly on the steering wheel, gazed in the back and noticed a look of despair on Roy's face. His immediate concern was whether the Austin Cambridge could face up to this rough terrain and if it could, for how long.

Approaching the border into Maribor, a wooden house bridged across the road, with a large Yugoslavian flag waving in the mild breeze. It hovered high above the security guard who was now making his way towards their car. The checkpoint process was seamless, just as it had been with all previous checkpoints.

As they passed through, none of them had any idea where they were going to spend the evening. Exhaustion was eating away in the minds and body, with Gurcharan struggling to keep his eyes focused on the road. The passengers in the back began drifting in and out of sleep, never managing to keep their eyes closed for long. Constant yawning was now having a negative effect on the concentration of the brothers.

Inder advised they needed to find a quiet spot and stop over for the night, as it was potentially dangerous to keep on the road. Since leaving Austria, they had spent a majority of the day in the car and it was proving their toughest experience to date. To make matters worse no accommodation enquiries had been made in advance; frankly they had no clue.

Often the radio would come to their salvation, but they struggled to find a suitable station to keep engaged long enough. When the radio was off, the silence made passing time even more difficult. All conversations had dried up.

Early evening quickly descended into darkness and this required even more concentration. It became hard to separate the road from the bumpy gravel either side, or even spot the turns up ahead. A few minutes later Gurcharan pulled the car to the side and into a lay-by. He peered outside and discovered the outline of two benches. Without even saying a word the brothers retrieved two blankets from the boot and curled up on the wooden surface. The strong smell of the chipped wood weaved its way through their nostrils.

With the car parked in front acting as a barrier, their eyes and mind drifted into a state of nothingness. So deep was the trance that they would have been forgiven for forgetting what country they were in. It was absolute silence all around them. This provided a hint of assurance as for the first time, the brothers were exposed to the outside darkness.

Just before nodding off, Inder and Gurcharan spoke of sleeping outdoors in India. These hard-wooden benches were no match for the traditional manji they had spent many a summer evening's sleeping on. Synthetic fibre rope was inter-woven tightly around four wooden legs to create a solid base on which to lie on.

While these benches were uncomfortable, they didn't have to fight off mosquitos as they did on that rooftop at home. The air here was much cleaner and kind, and their surroundings looked unspoilt even in the dark. With that thought, Gurcharan realised he was blabbering to himself, as Inder had long fallen asleep. Folding both his hands and using them for a pillow, he never noticed when he fell asleep himself.

As the first rays of the sun beamed onto the benches the brothers could feel its warmth radiating onto their backs. Glancing quickly at the car and then turning over, they sat upright to witness what was in front of them. They practically found themselves right up against a jungle. Exhaustion and the darkness meant they were unable to conduct their usual safety checks, and so marvelled at their luck of sleeping undisturbed in such a raw environment.

Both took a moment to absorb the scenery, and it was quite extraordinary. Moving closer to the edge, and in the distance, they could see some wildlife. There was a cheetah, a group of monkeys, and even a snake. It was fortunate that in this unprotected environment they had remained unharmed all night and not been attacked by one of these animals who may have been hunting for their next meal.

It wasn't long before the sounds of the jungle woke Roy, Sarita and Kunal who also now marvelled at their surroundings. Since his birth, Kunal had never been to a wildlife park in England. Close encounters with animals had been restricted to programmes on television, and so this open-air experience was a revelation for him.

Sarita savoured the moment as she watched Roy point out the animals to Kunal. To her, the road trip had come at a good time, enabling Roy to spend some quality time with their child. The pressure and stresses of life in England had begun to take its toll on their small family. The desire to achieve success by filling every recognisable hour with work, and to prove something to those back home, had reached a tipping point.

Inder clasped his hands in admiration of the beauty around them, but also for this moment. In truth, this was a stark contrast from the closed spaces they had experienced in previous destinations. Looking around he saw smiling faces, and for the first time some affectionate interaction between Kunal and his parents. While this ambience may not last between now and the remainder of the road trip, he felt small moments like this would keep them going.

Breakfast was heated in a pan on the stove ignited by an electric lighter. The cuisine of the morning being tinned beans and some bread which they had purchased during their stay in Austria. Feeling much fresher, preparations were made to get back onto the rough road as early as possible.

Leaving Maribor, they headed along the pebbly road with the occasional crunch of a large stone under the sturdy tyres. They hadn't travelled far when suddenly the road ahead was swamped in a thick fog. It looked as if someone had chopped it off. Visibility was very poor, and it was almost impossible to see anything in front.

Slowing the car so that it crept along at the pace of a snail seemed the most sensible course of action. Then out of nowhere a truck appeared in front of them. The dim back lights gave little time to react and they ploughed straight into the back, and making a loud thud. Seatbelts at the front avoided any serious injury but still couldn't stop the jolting of the necks. Roy had managed to restrain Kunal at the right time and Sarita pushed into the seat in front of her.

In that moment, Gurcharan noticed the entire contents of the roof rack slide down the windscreen and roll in front of them. Peering over he noticed some of the bags had slide under the truck. As everything become silent, the brothers realised just how close they were to a life-threatening incident. There were two metal rods pointing out from the back of the truck and were just inches away from the windscreen.

The brothers were afraid to leave the car. It wasn't just for the safety of everyone, but also reluctant to see the extent of the damage. They were certain this was the end of the road.

Is this the end of the road?

Despite the seriousness of the accident, there were no injuries as each one gave a nod of approval after a careful check. Luck and the robustness of the car had saved them from a potential disaster.

The Austin Morris Cambridge Estate had a long front wheelbase with lots of room from the tip of the bonnet to the engine. Without doubt it was due to this design that the impact had been minimised to just the outside. Everything remained motionless as the thick fog began to clear. With no sign of the driver moving from his truck, the brothers took the initiative and gingerly stepped out.

Lifting the bonnet and inspecting the engine, they found it had miraculously remained intact. Eventually, the driver of the truck came out ranting and raving in a language totally alien to them. He waved his hands frantically while shouting and widening his eyes which were red with fury. Inder and Gurcharan tried to remain calm while constantly checking over their shoulders at the passengers in the car.

To make matters worse, the local Police happened to arrive at the scene of the incident. A brief dialog took place between the officer and driver. Gurcharan gestured to Inder that something wasn't right here. They insisted in broken English while pointing to their badges, that the brown coloured foreigners follow them to the station. Suddenly, a state of panic crept in. Here they were, new to the country, and with no idea about the local people or their customs.

Inder and Gurcharan walked back to the car and consulted with Roy. There was nothing any of them could do and right now the most important thing was not to give the officers any excuse to become physical. Roy was immediately worried for Sarita and Kunal. The brothers assured him no harm would come to them.

The officers continued to shout instructions and Roy could see Kunal was visibly shaken by their behaviour. His concerns were heightened at the possibility of their car being confiscated. Such a scenario would leave them all but stranded and certainly put an end to their journey. There was no time to delve on the matter but rather trust their instincts.

Gurcharan and Inder collected the luggage off the road and strapped it back onto the roof rack.

What made them more nervous now was the casual conversation that was taking place between the truck driver and officers. Ushering a prayer, Gurcharan started the car and followed the Police into the unknown.

The Police station

Driving some ten miles they finally arrived at the station. Once again, the officers insisted that they all leave the car and come inside. Inder and Gurcharan's concerns now firmly sat with Sarita and Kunal, and Roy was bubbling up with frustration. The situation could erupt at any moment. They both knew they had to take control, remain calm, focused and work with the officers to come to some sort of compromise.

Being good citizens, the brothers had never brushed with the law and therefore never set foot inside a police station. However, growing up and watching Bollywood movies gave them some sense of what one looked like.

The double fronted beige coloured building stood proud against the morning sky. Parts of the facia had chipped away to expose the underlying brick. Surprisingly, there were no windows on the ground floor, just three arch shaped doors painted black. There was something harsh about this building, maybe a cruel history that Inder couldn't quite put his finger on, and it made him feel very uneasy.

Stepping through the door this station made those flaky ones in the movies look like a place of luxury. The darkness of the place aided by low lit light created a sinking feeling in Gurcharan's stomach. A coat of paint had long deserted the walls, with the existing paint work overwhelmed by damp. Large brown spots were dotted about the corners and resembled a sun-like image.

There was a stale smell lingering through the small office, which was lined with wooden benches against the walls. It reminded Inder of a school corridor outside the class, with a similar bench where the naughty children sat. They were all made to sit at one end of the room, while the officers again spoke to the angry truck driver.

The dialect was getting aggressive and the brothers' concerns were deepening. At this stage they had no idea what the outcome would be. Numerous scenarios swirled in their heads and none of them had a happy ending. Could the car be taken away? Were they all going to be asked to pay lots of money? They could all face jail if they couldn't afford to pay!

It wasn't long before the officers gestured to the waiting party by pointing fingers in their direction with a sharp wiggle. Roy shot up first, marching over, followed by Inder and Gurcharan. What followed was a heated exchange, with everyone blaming each other. The only English phrase the truck driver knew was *fault* and he kept repeating it in every sentence.

The ferocity of arguing wasn't getting Inder and Gurcharan anywhere, and the officers just smirked at each other whilst watching this scene unfold. They were obviously enjoying the predicament the visitors had found themselves in. The hand gestures were creating unnecessary tension.

Gurcharan glanced at the dusty clock on the wall, and it seemed like an age since their arrival, and exhaustion had kicked in. Mouths were dry, and the beautiful scenery of the morning wildlife was now a distant memory. This couldn't go on any longer and so the brothers made a bold decision to just stop communicating. They pulled out their wallets to show the officers, sending a message that they had no money.

A suspicion had arisen from the onset of how the police had conveniently arrived at the scene. On the way to the Police station Roy, Sarita, Inder and Gurcharan had guessed that this was a ploy to strip them of any money they had. To add further misery to the officer's devious plan, Inder gleefully offered the tins of food as a gesture of good will. With nothing else to offer, the exchanges fell silent. It's as if the wind had been knocked out of the local inhabitants.

Looking unimpressed and disappointed, the officers instructed Roy to fill out multiple forms, which asked the same information over and over again. In the meantime, Inder and Gurcharan ushered Sarita and Kunal into the car, ready for a swift get away in case the officers changed their minds.

No sooner had Roy sat himself back in the car, they sped off on the rocky road. Heading towards a town called Ptuj, the plan was to catch sight of locals who could point them in the right direction. Uncharacteristically Inder drove faster than normal, constantly checking the back mirror. There was no complaint from anyone because they wanted to put as much distance as possible from the crooked officers.

Finally, Inder caught sight of a sign welcoming visitors to Ptuj. On seeing the first person Gurcharan rolled down the window to ask for directions towards Bulgaria. With a hiss and scratch of the chin the man shouted back some instructions, but mostly pointing in different directions. What he manged to ascertain was that the border into Bulgaria was a couple of hours away. To continue that journey without a break would certainly invite trouble.

After the accident there was uncertainty around the long-term damage to the car. So far it was coping well but they could ill-afford a breakdown in the middle of this dusty and baron land.

Driving along a narrow road they found Ptuj to be a very colourful town. There was a cosy feeling to this place, with its houses bound together, and lined with brightly coloured sloping roofs. Spotting a small cafe, Inder parked beside a church, with a small plaque reading *Church of St George*. A chalkboard outside indicated a list of what was on today's specials menu, but they couldn't understand the language.

The moment they sat down in the terrace area, a waiter hurried along. Mimicking the sipping of a drink, he brought some water, empty glasses and a pot of black coffee. Since the accident and police interrogation none of them had eaten anything. Although the adults could have survived on fluid alone, there was Kunal to think about. Roy ordered a plate of vegetables and selection of cheeses with breads or **Hleb's** as the waiter pointed out. The weather was mild, and the air remained fresh, as it did in Maribor.

Whilst waiting for their food they noticed a group of men performing a dance on the opposite side of the road. A few of them had cowbells jangling from their belt, making ringing noises as they jumped up and down. Once the men finished their short rendition, they moved from house to house. Each time a member of the household would give them a donation. It seemed like pieces of fruit which the men carefully placed in their pouches.

The dancing amused Kunal and Sarita which was a welcome break from the torrid experience a little while back. Gurcharan noticed a wooden stick that one of the men was carrying which had something tied to it. The man was wearing a bright red mask with big black eyes, almost like the devil. A local person, whose English was surprisingly good, told them that the thing tied to the wooden stick was the skin of a hedgehog and that it was used to ward off evil spirits.

He continued, stating these men took it upon themselves to ensure bad spirits in the house or nearby street were warded off so as not to cause ill health and bad luck. Such events were commonplace around Yugoslavia, and especially to commemorate historical events. His tone dropped admitting that in local towns such as Ptuj some men had turned this into a small business enterprise. Any form of payment worked, whether this be food or money. The larger the donation the quicker the evil spirit could be dispelled. Rarely did a house resident refuse the giving of a donation from the fear of inviting even more bad luck.

Inder gestured to Gurcharan about what was unfolding in front of them, but Roy didn't quite follow the moment. In the brother's city, and in most cities across India, such rituals were commonplace too. Back home, it would be men dressed as women, often a social group referred to as hijras[11] who visited homes and businesses on occasions of celebration. They would arrive as a herd dancing and praying for continued success or growth. Payment was often money however if the recipient was wealthy enough, they may even present the hijras with expensive gifts.

These hijras would often dance and sing while bestowing blessings upon their recipients. A refusal to donate could result in curses being offered to the family. The fear of the unknown often planted a seed of doubt and rarely did anyone risk calling their bluff.

---

[11] In the Indian subcontinent, Hijra are eunuchs, intersex people, and transgender people

Inder mentioned hearing stories where the curse manifested itself into reality, resulting in extreme bad luck or even the loss of life. Roy seemed unconvinced in his response, stating that this was merely a scheme to make money by instilling fear into people.

The local man sat with the newly arrived visitors for a while, but more so intrigued by the brothers' attire and shiny beards. He too advised them that it was a long drive from this town to the border of Bulgaria. His advice was they stop somewhere outside of Sarajevo. He recommended a place called Banja Luka, an area with open spaces and camp sites where they could stop over for the evening.

The on-street entertainment couldn't mask the quality of the food that was offered in the cafe. The black coffee was light in taste, and the salad was slightly brown around the edges. The cheese had a strong taste to it. Kunal ignored the salad in favour of finishing off all the bread. Sarita had layered it with too much butter, much to the annoyance of Roy.

Saying their goodbyes, they were back on the road. Inder noticed Roy taking a momentary glance towards the church, placing two fingers to his chest and forehead. In none of the conversations had anyone spoken about faith. But Inder was intrigued. The question arose whether Roy was thanking God for getting them this far or praying for whatever lay ahead?

Thankful to leave the jungle, in one piece

The northern road from Ptuj to Banja Luka was not the smoothest however, offered spectacular scenery along the Vrbas Valley. It curved like a snake and driving required extreme caution and focus. 100 Km of persevered driving got them to the town of Banja Luka, taking several hours to negotiate.

Upon arriving it wasn't clear where these camp sites might be. Having spent the previous evening sleeping on the cusp of a jungle, and surrounded by wild animals, the brothers weren't too keen on further exposure. At the same time Sarita wasn't keen on spending another evening cramped in the car. The novelty had well and truly rubbed off.

Roy indicated he was willing to part with any accommodation costs and so asked the brothers to stop at the first hotel they could find. A nearby shopkeeper advised them that there were only two good hotels in the local area, the Bosna or the Palas. The latter would arrive first on their route into the centre of town.

Hotel Palas occupied most of the street, stretching around the corner. Its pale-yellow stonework was dated, a bit like those country manor houses on the back of magazines in England. Nevertheless, it was a huge step up from their previous accommodations. Flowing awnings lined the bottom floor of the building concealing shops selling clothes, food and chocolates.

As they all stepped inside, a dark grey lobby greeted them. This hotel was supposed to be one of the better ones which made Roy wonder what the sub-standard ones looked like. It was no surprise that rooms were available, this certainly wouldn't have appealed to the traveller passing through. Thankfully checking in was seamless with the person at reception well versed in English.

Later in the evening Roy treated everyone to dinner in the hotel. Inder and Gurcharan had tried their ample best to push back on the kind gesture but Roy was having none of it. This was his way of saying thanks for how the brothers handled the situation at the police station and getting away unharmed.

Feeling more at ease, the discussion centered very much on the incident from the morning. It was a stark reminder of the dangers that faced them as they ventured through the different countries. Today their journey was close to ending in utter disaster, and the realisation that without protection they were at the peril of the local inhabitants.

It was now even more vital to remain extra cautious and follow their intended route. Before they knew it, Europe would be a distant memory and the maps would no longer be of use. Without this they'd have to rely on the locals for directions.

It was straight to bed after dinner. The extra day's stay in Yugoslavia was the right decision, and to get some much-needed rest. More importantly, their car needed urgent attention to avoid the chance of something going wrong. But for now, no sooner had they reached their rooms the doors were shut tightly with the *do not disturb* sign left hanging on the doorknob.

Inder and Gurcharan carefully removed their turbans and stretched themselves on the single beds. They were springy and receptive to every movement. However, it was much better than the restricted space in the car. Just like on the jungle benches, no sooner had they rested their heads on the pillow it was total lights out.

In the morning, Roy and Sarita collected some additional food supplies from a small supermarket near the hotel. Food was running low and the route they had planned was heading into baron land. Such places would seldom be lined with bustling cafes and restaurants, so it was time to become self-sufficient again.

The hotel staff were kind enough to map out the shortest route to the Bulgarian border. The drive into Sarajevo took them along the River Miljačka, running under several bridges, with the vastness of the area catching Kunal's attention.

Sarajevo was a place where small rocks disappeared, and the roads now lined with beautiful lush green parks, gardens and orchards. In comparison Banja Luka was totally devoid of beauty. In hindsight Inder may have pushed himself to drive further the day before only to spend an evening here.

Sarajevo was a city entrenched in religious culture. Several mosques lined the streets as they drove through the city centre. A Turkish tower with Arabic letters as a clock face stood tall and proud next to Gazi Husref Beg's Mosque.

They discovered a little bit of England right there. A red double-decker bus like the one's found in London, bustling with commuters overtook them to perform a drop off. This was a rare sight, that in a place with strong traditional Turkish culture, there was room for some Westernisation.

Leaving Sarajevo, they headed towards Višegrad and across its famous bridge, a honey coloured stone construction with arches curving above them. There was no traffic in sight, and so Roy requested they stop to read a plaque on the parapet. The words inscribed read ***Bridge built by Mehmed Paša Sokolović in***

1571. Severely damaged by the Germans in 1943. Restored between 1949-52. Roy made a note of the information, studying it carefully and mumbling to himself. Inder was sure that he would be looking this up when he reached India.

The journey from Višegrad to Kruševac was filled with small stops for help with directions. Eventually they reached the last point in this vast country, Dimitrovgrad. This was the frontier town before Bulgaria, surrounded by road, river, railway and with vast plains of land and forest.

It seemed like an age since they had left Banja Luka to head to the borders of Bulgaria. The long drive had tested their concentration and so Dimitrovgrad seemed like a sensible stop. Here the sounds of crunching tyres alerted them to the rocky nature of the road, the tarmac had disappeared a while back.

Signs of fading light posed its own potential problems and so a brief rest was in order. As the rocks settled behind them, the cloud of dust could not hide the mixed emotions that everyone was experiencing.

They were absolutely shattered and not sure what energy force was spurring them on.

Twenty-four hours earlier they had set foot into Yugoslavia and brushed with its stark wildlife, demonstrating such beauty.

However no sooner had that memory began to sink in, they were reminded of the truck incident and it over-shadowed all that was good about this place.

1964 - Love develops

It was a busy morning in the Chhatwal household as preparations were being made for the arrival of Charanjit and her family. Their courtship had been steady but frequent, albeit under the careful supervision of elders. Popping out for lunchtime snacks, walking around the local bazaar, and the reluctant touching of hands was just some of the moments they shared.

By their standard this courtship had been long and fruitful, with no questions being asked. However, with each meeting an expectation arose. This wasn't an expectation on the part of Gurcharan or Charanjit but from the local community who had witnessed them together on several occasions.

When the time was right, they both discussed a future together with their parents, and the response was swift. The heads of both families wasted no time in approving the bond of marriage. This was now adult territory and as per tradition, Inder and Charanjit would have little say in the proceedings.

Surprisingly Gurcharan took longer than usual to get ready. His beard was firmly pressed down by a black nylon cloth. The cloth was wrapped around his chin and knotted at the top of his head, tighter than usual. This was a common look for all the men in Gurcharan's house. The cloth had the job of holding the beard in place. After a while the cloth would be removed to reveal a firm and impeccable hold.

While Gurcharan was overjoyed at the prospect of seeing Charanjit, and officially cementing their relationship, he was sad that Inder was not here to share in this moment. Gurcharan couldn't even begin to imagine how Inder was feeling, being so far away and not able to share in this joyful occasion. But he knew his brother would be ringing home in the evening to ensure everything went ok.

The afternoon sun spread its rays across the veranda which was now congested with a myriad of chairs. They were equally parted so as to make clear distinctions between the host family and their guests. A rectangular shaped wooden table separated Gurcharan and Charanjit, who in brief moments exchanged glances. The air was awash with chatter and laughter, but Charanjit struggled to smile, her nerves getting the better of her.

Hot cups of chai were consumed with sweetmeats. Surjan Singh talked with humble pride of his other son Inder working in England and supporting the family. Mr Nanda nodded in approval, citing that it was important to take such opportunities.

Dialog amongst the families helped break the ice and it was time to proceed with the main event. As the focus turned to Gurcharan and Charanjit, Mr Nanda placed some items of clothing, a long red cloth to be used for the turban and 51 Rupees into Gurcharan's lap. This seal of approval confirmed Gurcharan and Charanjit's engagement.

Those in the room hugged each other to signify the coming together of two families as one. Gurcharan took another glance in the direction of Charanjit, and though she had her head down, he noticed a smile.

It's getting dusty

There was no border security to welcome a damaged car and five exhausted passengers as they rolled into Bulgaria. The small rocks ended, and they were once again on smooth surface and less impacting for the car. The drama that had unfolded in Yugoslavia resulted in a quiet journey, even the break in Dimitrovgrad hadn't helped encourage any conversation.

It seemed there was so much on their minds, but no one dared to bring up the subject. The silence was finally broken by the most trivial of things, the road signs! It looked as if a child has scribbled something. There were letters with lines through them, and some back to front. It was impossible to tell what direction they were heading in, let alone if it was the right one. Gurcharan decided to throw caution to the wind and continue heading along the narrow road.

A sweet scent made its way through the car vents, *roses* said Sarita. Either side of the road they noticed fields of rose bushes, each beautifully lined in a diagonal pattern. Driving further on, they noticed women carefully picking the roses and placing them into baskets brimming to the top.

Gurcharan pulled over to ask for directions, as he was reluctant to continue driving in case they got totally lost. Sarita nominated herself to make the enquiry. Gurcharan was relieved as he wasn't too keen on approaching the women himself. Not aware of the local customs, the last thing he wanted to do was to offend anyone and risk a reprisal.

Sarita approached a young woman dressed in a bright red floral dress; she was almost camouflaged with the background. Her golden hair shone bright in the morning sun, with short pigtails either side. However, unlike the other women she wasn't wearing the white head cover, but a garland made of the very pink roses she was picking.

Sarita was careful in her approach, not being sure how much, if any, English the lady would understand. Exchanging greetings, the woman nodded and pointed in a certain direction when asked about Sofia, it seems they were on the right track.

Sarita continued to ask about possible camp sites, the woman blushed with disappointment in not understanding her. She glanced in the direction of a man who was now hastily making his way towards them both. He claimed to be the farm supervisor and showed some willingness to help them. Roy opened the back door to come out but Sarita waved him away. She was in her element and didn't need any help.

The supervisor was smartly dressed but not so articulate with his English. However, he managed to convey the necessary instructions. It was then that Sarita ushered Roy out so he could make a note in his book. The supervisor then walked over to inspect their car, shaking his head as he mumbled to himself. Inder arched his eyebrows at this gesture and shot a half-hearted look back in the supervisor's direction.

Thanking the supervisor and the lady with rose garlands, the car sped off in the direction of Sofia. Inder unfolded a piece of paper scribed with a list of local garages. It was kind of the supervisor to share this information after he had inspected the car.

Roy divulged in an observation, commenting on the types of people they had come across to date. This most recent engagement was a good example of how some people went out of their way to help strangers. He delved a little deeper into his own experiences of running a business. Having moved to England and being strangers, no one had taken the time to help them. A certain bitterness echoed through Roy's words. Inder and Gurcharan waited for more clarity but it never came.

Inder shared his own experience of when he arrived in England, and how Chanan Singh embraced him. If it wasn't for Chanan Singh who knows what would have become of him – it was a blessing in disguise. Sarita complimented Inder for his humble nature, while not forgetting the kindness of others.

A campsite on the outskirts of Sofia was the ideal spot for the evening. Roy momentarily stepped out of the car to negotiate a rate for the night. Straight after that they headed to a local garage.

Earlier Roy had questioned the need to have the car checked. If it was still driving ok, then maybe they could make it all the way. However, Gurcharan pushed back, advising an inspection was the very least they should do. With the road potentially getting rougher, taking no action could jeopardise the rest of their journey.

The road leading to the garage was narrow, barely enough for two cars to pass, and was lined with large boulders either side. Beyond the dusty boulders sat banks of patchy land devoid of rain. The dust flew up and stained the car windows. It was a warm morning and the car was heating up, but no one opened the windows from fear of the musky smell outside.

Beige land was the backdrop to the garage. A few cars were sitting silently with their bonnets open for surgery. No sooner had they approached the rusty iron doors that a short stout man walked over and started inspecting the car. Upon his initial inspection the man's advice was that while he couldn't replace specific parts, he would be able to apply some minor repairs.

The car could be patched well enough to provide much needed resistance to the road ahead. Roy was comfortable with the proposal, but the sticking point was how to pay seeing he had no Bulgarian currency.

Roy offered to pay in pounds, but this was declined in favour of dollars. Unfortunately, none of them had dollars with them. Even when Roy showed his credit card it was swiftly waved away. The further they moved away from mainland Europe the less likely it was to use card as a form of payment.

As an awkward silence surrounded them all, Sarita piped up with an idea. It was a long shot, but they had no other option. She proposed that they offer the stockings as a form of payment. The boot had a bag brimming with stockings of different colours. Roy was unsure whether this would work and reluctant in case the man took offense.

Sarita quizzed Roy on whether he had any other ideas to which he fell silent. Sensing options being limited, she half-heartedly opened the bag to reveal the contents. Expecting the worse they were surprised when the man started to look at the different colours with a keen eye. Smiling in their direction, he nodded in approval and happily took a large bundle as payment.

Todor, the mechanic and garage owner estimated a couple of hours to carry out the repairs. The fact he could start right away was a bonus however, with nowhere to go the passengers had to pass time right here. With limited seating in the garage, added by the strong smell of oil, they all chose to remain in the car.

Warm air circled inside, and they had no option but to roll down the windows and hope for a breeze of cool air from somewhere. When either passenger did get a moment to doze off, they would be woken up by the sound of knocking or loud whistling. Occasionally, the cool breeze floated through the open windows providing momentary relief.

Giving up on catching any sleep, Inder and Gurcharan turned their attention to Kunal. He had remained passive over the last day or so, and the brothers were mindful that maybe the police station incident was still looming large in his mind. Inder asked Kunal what he had enjoyed so far about their journey. Shy at first but with encouragement from his mother, he talked about the animals in the jungle and how they made different sounds. His favourite animal were the monkeys because he liked how they could jump from one tree to another.

The interaction continued for a short while until the brothers ran out of things to ask. Once again, the silence crept in. Gurcharan noticed that Kunal remained close to his mother, and not so much to Roy.

Several hours later, and what seemed like an eternity, the repairs were finished. Their next stop was a petrol station and much needed nourishment for the car. Once again, they tried their luck and managed to purchase fuel in exchange for stockings. It seemed for now, bartering was their only option until Roy could acquire the local currency.

Some six hours later Gurcharan pulled up at the camp site, with everyone exhausted and a little fed up. It was an uneventful evening of tinned food and tired conversations. No one was in the mood to offload what was on their mind. The brutal reality of the road now faced them! This experience was in danger of fast becoming a chore.

The roads felt endless and without a map to guide them, they felt vulnerable. Maybe it was a good idea not to talk about this. They needed to remain positive ahead of their drive to Turkey, all seven hundred miles of it.

It's not just the car that needs repairs

It hadn't been a comfortable night's sleep for any of them, with limbs feeling stiff. Their stomachs were rumbling as last night's meal was not filling enough.

Today's drive was going to be their longest, and most physical. Mental preparation therefore was important. Gurcharan had read in the material sent by the RAC, that camp sites across Europe were manned by an onsite ranger. The ranger here had been very helpful this morning. He managed to organise warm cups of tea for all of them and some milk for Kunal. A small wooden lodge housed some basic kitchen essentials and so they all polished off a couple of thickly buttered toasts.

The brothers re-told the episode of how they paid for car repairs in the form of stockings. The ranger found this most amusing. Roy offered something for the inconvenience, but the ranger refused and wished them well on the next leg of their journey.

Before parting, he handed over a small selection of books written in English so they could keep themselves occupied. The books were largely based on the history of Bulgaria and insights into its culture. This show of kindness restored some faith in the passengers who were very much humbled.

It was 10:00am local time as they drove through Sofia via its large roads, multiple cross ways, and past its government buildings and historic monuments. Sofia had a similar feel to France and Austria. The novelty of being tourists and partaking in sightseeing was wearing off. Instead, Roy took the opportunity to pick up one of the books and start reading through it.

Every so often he would share some of the knowledge he had just acquired from a chapter. There was the Crimean War which lasted for three years and saw the Russian Empire lose to Britain, France, Sardinia and the Ottoman Empire. It was also one of the first conflicts which used modern warfare technology such as naval shells.

He read aloud a chapter about Bulgaria's independence in 1908, some sixty years ago. The discussion then drifted onto India's independence in 1947. The bloodshed that followed on from one of largest mass migrations of communities touched on raw memories. Some twenty years on, the effects were still fresh on all their minds but nothing further was said.

A few hours later they were driving along vast farmlands that stretched for miles. The air was fresh and the silence outside was welcoming. In that moment the brothers felt like they had whizzed back into Panjab. The lands filled with crops against grassy banks. Stopping the car, they plucked a few vegetables and fruit from one of the farms while whispering a prayer for forgiveness.

As they passed the empty border into Turkey, signs of local people became apparent. Roy was relived and proud of how resolute the Austin Cambridge had been in dealing with the uneven and often unforgiving terrain. He also paid compliments to the brothers for their exceptional care and focus behind the wheel. The mood had improved following their recent experiences in Yugoslavia, and a perked up Kunal was a good signal.

Going through cold Turkey

From their research, Inder and Gurcharan knew Turkey was a large country to travel across, so they braced themselves for another long period in the car.

As always, their first objective was to locate the camp site they had made a note of during early planning. Gurcharan estimated it would take them around two hours to reach the outskirts of Istanbul. The estimation was based on what he had learnt during this road trip, often calculating speed and distance travelled to get an idea. If nothing else, it helped set expectations for the next pit stop.

The camp site was located off the main road they had been driving along. At the foot of the entrance was a large board with Turkish writing on it. The inscription looked professional with a logo next to it, indicating that it was an approved camping area. The only bit of information they didn't understand was the number 50. Roy commented this may have meant 50 pitch areas or spaces.

Driving through the narrow posts, the vastness of the land surprised them. A pebbly path ran alongside the greenest grass they had seen amongst all the other camp sites. Parking up everyone stretched their legs and walked around the site to see what was on offer. Roy was relieved to see a restaurant with a board outside describing what looked like the daily specials.

Entering the restaurant, he quickly walked back out. Language was a problem as no one spoke English, and there was very little choice of food on offer. Inder and Gurcharan assessed their options, and with nothing nearby for food recommended they leave this camp site and drive on. Roy and Sarita were apprehensive at first but trusted the brother's judgement. Bundling back into the car they drove on further along the main road.

Noticing a petrol station with the large board reading *Petrol Ofisi*, they pulled in to fuel up. A rather inquisitive looking man walked towards their car while Inder was re-fuelling, and pointing to his turban, uttering the word ***Indian***. Inder nodded in agreement, and they engaged in conversation. Roy walked in to make payment while Inder replayed back the conversation.

Inder mentioned to the stranger the difficulty they had experienced at the last camp. The man advised him there was a Christian community residing in Istanbul, and just a short drive from the petrol station. He recommended a camp site nearby which was used by the local community who were well versed in English. What seemed like a despondent situation a while back turned into a chance opportunity. Once again, the kindness of the local people helped the passengers on their journey.

As indicated, and just a few miles later they arrived at the next camp site. The board outside had the number 150 in big letters. This was much bigger and busily housed caravans and estate cars.

Instantly they could sense a more upbeat feel about this place. Lots of campers had perched themselves outside their vehicles, with some huddled around makeshift tables and others sprawled across blankets. Picnics were in full flow with families chatting away. Some read books while others just enjoyed the warm air while sleeping.

Their excitement of pitching up was short lived. Inder noticed the repairs conducted in Bulgaria were already showing some signs of concern. The right wing had come lose and one side of the front bumper had dropped a few inches. Something needed to be done, and they needed guidance from a local. The camp ranger advised there was a garage just a few miles from the site and seemed confident they could re-patch the repairs.

While this was good news, it brought about an immediate frustration. Not having a tent was proving to be a hinderance. Ideally Sarita and Kunal could have stayed at the camp site, but with no cover they felt exposed. Roy regretted not packing a tent or covering of some kind, even some chairs. The on-site cafe was a squeeze and the smell of food had put Sarita off.

The brothers knew exactly how frustrating it was becoming. During long periods and being wedged together often resulted in pins and needles, or joints stiffening up. They'd be out of the car for brief moments, trying to bring some relief. However, the sensation wouldn't last long, and they'd be back in that fixed position again.

Inder couldn't help but notice the recent frown across Sarita's forehead. If she kept that up, they'd surely be a permanent line from one side of her head to another. There was a point of no return for each of the passengers which they had all passed a long time ago, however, Sarita was now struggling to see the end.

He dared not ask for the fear of getting more than he bargained for. No sooner had they all stretched and sampled the fresh air that all huddled back into the car and headed towards another garage in hope they could get a permanent fix.

The reality of the road kicks in

Just as the camp ranger had instructed them, the smooth road turned dusty. Inder swung the car into the entrance leading to a dust covered metal shack. Roy and Gurcharan approached a slim looking man smelling of engine oil. His piercing blue eyes narrowed on them through his blackened face.

To their surprise, Mehmet wasted no time in pointing out the patch up repairs that had taken place beforehand. Not being busy, he assured them of doing a better job and servicing the car at the same time. Once again, they were fortunate repairs could be carried out instantly however, they had no option but to wait around.

Sarita huffed in frustration once more. There was nothing nearby that they could walk to as the garage was remotely tucked away. While this meant sitting around, it was another opportunity to talk about themselves. Not that they hadn't done much talking at all, but those conversations had awkward silences, often pauses for thought without delving any deeper.

The seating area in the garage was made up of redundant car seats carefully placed on a pile of large wooden boards. The coffee table was a cut off roof with spots of rust that resembled the back of a cheetah. The creative nature of their surrounding lightened the mood and encouraged the conversation.

Inder and Gurcharan spoke of their family back in India, something they hadn't discussed much during the journey. Even though rocky roads still lay ahead, they could sense home wasn't too far away. Whether Roy and Sarita felt the same was a different story.

The smells of their city would consume their senses each time thoughts travelled back home. The brothers were hopeful their family would be relieved to see them. While there would be hugs and blessings, it would certainly be followed by a stiff telling off for driving so far. In their youthful thinking they had embraced this adventure but maybe overlooked the emotions and trepidation their parents must have been going through.

Sounds of hunger rang through their bellies and glasses of water were not suffice. Kunal slept soundly against the noise of the hammering and banging. It wasn't the same for the brothers who kept dropping in and out of sleep, often catching Roy and Sarita engaged in intense conversation.

Having been confined together for over a week, it remained a mystery on what was going on between the two of them. The confusion existed because Roy and Sarita's personal journey in England spoke of good teamwork and success. Yet the brothers had witnessed moments of disconnect. Maybe they were reading too much into this, it could be the nerves of reaching home and walking into the unknown.

Time passed quickly, and the wait hadn't been as painful as first anticipated. Inspecting the car, Roy was pleased with the work that had been carried out. He'd been keeping an eye on proceedings in between his conversations. Surprisingly, the garage owner had the means to accept payment by card. Just as well because the stockings were in short supply and they hadn't discussed payment on arrival.

Leaving a small trail of dust behind them they sped off towards the camp. The afternoon had now fast turned into evening. Behind them darkness had shrouded the surroundings of the engine oil fragranced garage.

Back at the camp site they had some assurance their car was mechanically reborn for the remainder of the journey. What surfaced very soon was the hunger, and they had to eat something before stomach cramps settled in. But once again obtaining food was a challenge due to the language barrier. This was, of course, a disappointment as the reason they came here was because of an English-speaking community, but where had they all gone?

There was a small lodge on the camp site which had a kitchen, and the camp ranger assisted the family as best he could. All the meat was Halal and so the passengers were reluctant to take that option. Small bowls of salad sat in a see-through fridge, but the lettuce leaves were turning brown and therefore not so appealing. Unable to acquire a hearty meal, they all closed the evening on fruit.

Strong cups of tea with slices of bread was the order of the morning. Sarita had managed to acquire some jam from the onsite shop and layered the bread with it for Kunal. He winced when taking a bite as the taste was very different to what he was used to. They were still hungry from last night but didn't want to spend any more time lurking around the site. Next up was the drive to Ankara, Turkey's capital.

Road signs were non-existent which meant stopping at regular intervals to ask for directions. Driving through the mountainous terrain exposed them to the most spectacular views. As the beautiful sceneries appeared one after the other the mood in the car improved. Roy and Sarita took turns in showing Kunal the mountains against the blue sky. But the dust never left them and made its way inside the car every time a window rolled down. Sarita had resorted to putting a chunni[12] over her and Kunal's face to stop the dust from sticking to them.

Apart from stopping for a comfort break, and the brothers swapping over, they adamantly kept going. The warm weather lifted slightly as they arrived some six hours later into the city of Ankara. The opening arms of the capital brought with it exhaustion and desperation, boredom and long periods of silence. In a nutshell they had *hit the wall*.

Ankara arrived, and it was yet another camp site, and another patch of land full of residents who didn't speak much English. Thankfully there was a cafe which offered a small selection of good quality hot food, and much-needed fuel for tired arms, legs and backs.

For the evening, Inder and Gurcharan opted to sleep on the sofas in the camp site lodge. There was no charge as long as they didn't help themselves to the contents of the fridge. The moment their heads touched the rough fabric of the sofa, a deep trance took

---

[12] A Chunni is a long scarf that is worn on top of an Indian dress by women

them fast along the dusty roads and somewhere close to home.

Time to connect, with faith and a friend

It was amazing what a good nights' sleep could do for a person. Everyone was up early with renewed determination. It wasn't easy finding their way out of Ankara due to limited information and no maps. After an hour of driving, turning back, and trying another route they managed to find the main road leading them towards their next destination, Iran.

The border crossing on the Turkish side was manned by men dressed in military uniforms. As they slowly approached the checkpoint, the guards were less inclined to check paperwork as the brothers waved their visas and passport. A few metres further over the hill, they were greeted at the Iranian border crossing and subjected to a bit more scrutiny. The tall proud men had mixed emotions on their faces.

Finally, they passed through a yellow tattered sign scribed with the words *welcome to Iran*. The dry rocky surface made a crunching sound on the tyres. Small patches of grass, barely able to grow, lined the sides while accompanied by more banners. These banners marked the inauguration of the Shah of Iran, Mohammed Reza Pahlavi.

Driving along, they noticed small pockets of locals who were either celebrating or staring back at them with grim faces. The passengers were totally unaware of the history that had led to this historical event for the Iranian people. However, what was certain was they had to safely navigate their way through and onto the next checkpoint.

Inder's friend Jagthar had been a great help when they had met in Switzerland. However, Inder also had another friend who had been living in Iran for some years. Before leaving Slough, he had been in contact with this friend to share his plans. Seeing that their route passed through Iran it made sense to stop over and meet up. Inder had estimated it would take two weeks to reach his friends country.

The dust and rocks seemed to follow them here too and it felt as if they'd never left Turkey. In that vast country the road delivered a stark message of how mentally and physically challenging the journey had become. Yet it remained a miracle that their car hadn't suffered a single puncture on these roads. Like the car their will power wasn't totally deflated but was flirting on the edges of being so.

The lack of road signs again proved a challenge, and Inder wasn't sure whether they'd find their meeting point in Iran's capital city, Tehran. They headed to Tabriz where dusty roads became smooth tarmac, and an open gate to the industrial hub of the country.

There was a real cosmopolitan feel about the city which had a very western look to it. They had just enough time to stop and marvel at the Blue Mosque, with its intricate tile work and Islamic calligraphy. A local tour guide, seated on the pavement, sprung into life as they came closer. Gurcharan politely waved the guide away, telling him they were only stopping momentarily. Not to be deterred he told them he wasn't interested in any money but happy to give them an insight.

With a beaming smile he told them the Blue Mosque was constructed in 1465 by order of Jahan Shah, a ruler of the Kara Koyunlu. It was then reconstructed following a major earthquake in the 18th century. Many of the walls still had missing tiles.

Inside, the brick domes reached halfway before being overshadowed by the beautiful blue arches with Arabic inscription on them. Prayer halls were empty at this moment, and the green velvet mats lay silent in anticipation of the congregation.

Thanking the guide and apologising for having nothing to give him in return, they left Tabriz behind. After a steady drive for a couple of hours the passengers arrived in Tehran. Their checkpoint was a Gurdwara, which happened to be quite near Inder's friends house. It was also the only one in Tehran.

Bhai Ganga Singh Sabha Gurdwara stood on the corner of the street, opposite a hospital. There was a public telephone inside the hospital to where Inder headed to call his friend Tejinder. At the sound of his voice Tejinder was overjoyed to hear that they were ok and had made the effort to pay him a visit. Making a note of the route to his house, Inder hung up the phone and happily walked back to the car.

Gurcharan gestured to Inder that they go to the Gurdwara. It was the first time since leaving Slough they'd seen the tall orange flagpole with the Sikh symbol waving proudly, the Nishaan Sahib. By its very tradition the Sikh faith welcomed people from all faiths and backgrounds and so Gurcharan asked Roy if he and his family wanted to come.

They all stepped into the Gurdwara to pay their respects and be grateful for making it this far. Since leaving Slough, this had been the first opportunity for the brothers to hear the Holy words uttered inside the small divan hall. As they both sat crossed legged, the message from the Sikh Holy book, the Guru Granth Sahib Ji was one of assurance and encouragement. The brothers were mentally and physically exhausted, but the calmness and peace of this moment had a profound effect on them.

As the priest finished reading, they all partook in a small prayer. Back in the car, Roy commented on how radiant the brothers looked, and he was right, a renewed level of energy now flowed through them.

The narrow road leading to Tejinder's house was lined with three storey homes, each with decaying brick work crying out for colour that had long deserted them. Tejinder's house was no different, a modest looking property amongst a busy colony of people and animals roaming the street. Both friends embraced each other upon arrival, it had been a very long time since they last met back in India.

After being introduced to the rest of the family, a humble request was made for Sarita to wear the traditional Muslim dress. Although laws were a little relaxed on what women could wear, public appearance was still under scrutiny, especially in their colony.

That evening, everyone was treated to the hospitality of which they had not experienced before. Observing local customs, Tejinder insisted they all sit on the floor to eat. The food was a blend of Iranian cuisine including lamb, chicken, okra, onion flavoured rice with potatoes and rumali roti, something they hadn't seen or tasted before.

Sitting so closely together to eat reminded Inder and Gurcharan of times back home. Regardless of whatever time everyone got home they would all eat together. On one occasion, their sister had returned late from college as she was preparing for exams. Upon arriving home, she found that not a single family member had eaten; it was a ritual well observed. The thought also made them feel sad, that many evenings had flown by where they had not eaten together.

For Roy and his family, the pattern of work and long hours resulted in often eating alone. Therefore, this was a new experience for all of them, and long overdue. But it wasn't just today as for the last two weeks the passengers of the car had eaten together. It didn't matter what they ate or how little they had between them; it was just a nice feeling. Opening up to the rest of the family Roy commented that the habit of eating together was something he'd embrace going forward.

As Inder and Gurcharan enjoyed the food they carefully observed a drastic change in Roy's mood. His involvement and engagement in conversations with Tejinder and his family amazed them both. He spoke in more detail about his background and work, with Sarita feeling more comfortable to converse with the women. After dinner Kunal left his parents to sit with Tejinder's youngest daughter who had him drawing a picture. The calm ambience relaxed the general mood and in a long time everyone felt at ease. The ups and downs of the last two weeks had been worth realising this moment, and they weren't even home yet.

Barriers begin to fall, the mystery clears

The morning broke with the sound of prayers being bellowed over loudspeakers. Towering above the houses and attached to a steel pole they demanded everyone's attention. Tejinder and his family were of Sikh origin however, living in an Islamic country, observed its rules and regulations closely as possible.

The rest of the family were slowly waking up and following their normal routine. One of Tejinder's daughters sat perched in light blue jeans and white t-shirt, reading a book while sipping hot black tea. Then disappearing into a room, she returned covered head to toe in a black cotton burka.

Pulling up her veil she revealed a cheeky smile, then revealing her jeans. She loved to dress in the latest fashion but was fearful that anything on show would get her into trouble. Unknown to the brothers, this was further evidence of traditional Iran battling against the wave of western ideals that the young generation had started to grip onto.

The peaceful surroundings of Tejinder's house provided an ideal opportunity to spend the next few days relaxing. The strip of houses locked together provided limited space to walk around however, there was a small shared area available for all the neighbours to meet freely. Sarita and Kunal decided to stay indoors, while Roy, Inder and Gurcharan took the opportunity to sample some of the local atmosphere.

It was a warm morning and walking through the streets they noticed onlookers so were not sure whether it was them or Roy they were focusing on. As the three of them sat down, a local tea staller approached with some haste. With three small glasses balanced on a wooden tray, each was full to the brim with hot fragrant tea. He was happy to see new faces in town and so as a gesture of good will and hospitality, offered them on the house. Sipping slowly, Roy spoke openly for the first time.

His proposal of marriage to Sarita had not been accepted by either of the families many years ago. His voice deepened with awkward pauses. They were both educated, shared common interests but it wasn't enough to meet her family's expectations. This frustrated Roy's parents and they declined the whole proposal. Even when there was hope of reconciliation, out of spite and stubbornness both sets of families dismissed all possibilities.

In a moment of defiance, and something they both regretted, Roy and Sarita eloped and came to England. A year later Kunal had blossomed into their lives but marriage still eluded them. Roy's motivation was that he wanted to show both families the accomplishments they had achieved. For him, the Austin Cambridge was a symbol of that success.

Gurcharan was surprised at Roy's statement, hoping he was going to mention Kunal being their biggest achievement. Roy knew they would be scolded on many of the decisions they had taken, but he was determined to finally get married back home, and with the blessings of the families.

The brothers valued this personal insight, and paid tribute to Roy and Sarita's bravery. It was an achievement coming to a foreign country in search of work, but also with the motivation to prove a point. Together the couple soldiered on despite not having any blessings from their respective parents.

The evening passed with another wonderful meal, and with youngsters talking about their day at work or school. In turn the brothers took the lead on sharing their experiences of being on the road. Sarita interjected to speak of the people they met and strange customs they witnessed. As they talked about each country they passed through, the excitement grew on the faces of their audience, but also accompanied by a glimmer of regret in their eyes.

For them, the truth was that a lack of opportunities here in Iran meant they would have little chance to taste such experiences. Jobs were few and far between, pay was poor, and they wouldn't be able to save up enough.

The reality was their chances of leaving Iran to work abroad were exceptionally low. Conversations went long into the night, and the passengers of the Austin Cambridge momentarily forgot about the road trip ahead.

A surprising decision was made in the early hours not to travel to Afghanistan as planned. It wasn't that they wouldn't go at all, but just not today. This was partly down to Tejinder's humble request to stay another day. Tejinder and his family had also become very attached to their guests and welcomed this distraction.

For this reason, there was no early morning rise, and everyone slept in for a change. So deep was the sleep that not even the sound of morning prayers could disrupt the trance. Inder apologised for any inconvenience caused by this extended stay however, their hosts were not one bit bothered.

After a hearty breakfast Tejinder accompanied the brothers with Roy and his family to the local town to do some shopping. It wasn't a big town by any stretch however, it was noisy and bustling with local traders and tourists. The local dialect of Farsi was alien to them all, but the style of trading and bartering excited Inder and Gurcharan very much.

Cramped into a small space the sounds of chatter and music resembled chaos like that of India. What differentiated the traders here to back home was how passionate they were. Seeing none of them had local currency, Tejinder gladly offered to pay for any items. In return the brothers gave him some Sterling, but not before Tejinder refused countless times. Gurcharan purchased a Persian ornament for the family back home. While there was nothing devious about this, he hoped the sight of a Persian gift may lesson any potential scolding they were going to receive.

Early evening Gurcharan and Inder took it upon themselves to cook for everyone. With some cooking skills acquired from back home, and some from England, they managed to delight everyone with a selection of dishes. With the help of Tejinder's wife they even learned how to make a romali roti. It was another insightful evening filled with debate and stories. To close the evening Tejinder's wife sang a few classical songs, and this reminded Inder of Veena.

Before retiring to bed the brothers gifted each of Tejinder's children with some money. This was an age-old Indian custom and one that Tejinder himself could not refuse. The last few days had felt like a holiday and they were all totally relaxed and rejuvenated.

It was a tearful parting the next day, with the warmth shown by Tejinder and his family something they would never forget. A box of sweets was handed to Kunal as was custom and all were blessed with a safe journey to their respective homes. Thus, began the night drive into Afghanistan.

1964 - A new face?

A year had passed from that first night in England. Inder had formed strong relationships within the community and applied a hard work-ethic in his job. But he often felt alone and longed being united with family; he missed them dearly.

He often wrestled with the idea of whether he could get a family member to come over and join him. If this was even possible, who would he ask back home? The memories of separation were still fresh in the minds of his parents. There was also the question of whether there was enough room to house another Chhatwal. If there was to be anyone, then it would be Gurcharan. So, with this in mind Inder took on his next challenge.

He was performing well at work and his experiences in England had been relatively positive. He was optimistic that if carefully planned, and with the right guidance Gurcharan's move to England could become a reality. However, he was reluctant to mention anything to his brother until absolutely certain.

The first step was to apply for a work voucher[13]. But the chances of success were limited if he remained with his current employer. The position he held at work wasn't of a high enough status, and opportunities for promotion were hard to come by if you were of colour. While he was on good working terms with his non-Indian colleagues, they were not part of the management circle and didn't have the necessary influence.

Inder made the bold step of changing his job. He successfully found work with a company called POLYSIS as a mechanical engineer. The company had international credibility as manufacturers of conveyer belts and therefore provided an ideal opportunity for him to progress through the ranks. It was a huge risk because he was new and had to build his own reputation from the start. However, he immediately found the culture welcoming, and one where hard work was praised and rewarded.

Several months passed and Inder continued to apply himself to the amazement of one of the directors. The director was impressed with Inder, and had huge admiration for the fact that being the only turban worker, nothing seemed to faze him. A mutual

---

[13] 1962 Commonwealth Immigration Act stipulated that all Commonwealth passport holders wishing to work in the UK needed to apply for a work voucher.

respect formed and led to a strong friendship being established between the two. It was not usual practice for a director to sit with his team of workers and take lunch. But not in the case of Inder and they would spend many a lunch breaks learning more about each other's cultures.

As Inder grew confident of his position, he sought the guidance of Chanan Singh about Gurcharan. Chanan Singh advised that Inder should approach this director in the first instance about a work voucher. Inder seemed reluctant at first but realised that this approach would speed up the process.

Thinking back to the first day he met Inder, Chanan Singh marvelled at the progress he had made since arriving. It was therefore an easy decision for him, he told Inder not to worry about accommodation, and that they would come to some sort of arrangement.

It took a couple of weeks for Inder to build up the courage, but he finally approached his director to request a work voucher. When the director delivered his decision a few days later, it came as a total shock. He was happy to arrange for and guarantee the work voucher. The trust that Inder had instilled into their friendship, and the integrity with which he worked spoke volumes about his character.

When everything was in place, a doubt crept into Inder's mind. Would Gurcharan want to come to England? Maybe he had made too bold an assumption that his parents wouldn't have an issue. Whatever the outcome, he was going to find out very soon.

1964 - It's decision time

During their period of courtship, word came from England that Inder was keen on Gurcharan joining him. Going to England would mean leaving a perfectly good job, and more importantly running the risk of jeopardising his relationship with Charanjit. But equally important was what impact this request would have on their parents.

Surjan Singh was missing Inder despite the frequent correspondences. How would he take to having another one of his son's move away from the family? What impact would this have financially, socially and emotionally?

But, Gurcharan also recognised it was an opportunity worth considering, seeing how well his brother had blossomed there. Not wishing to focus too much on the subject for now, he decided to wait on the outcome of Inder's efforts before mentioning anything to his father and Charanjit.

The time between Gurcharan finding out and Inder finally contacting him flew by in an instant. While it was good news that everything was in place with regards to the voucher, it also escalated the growing feeling of trepidation within Gurcharan. Inder would make provisions to purchase the ticket for his flight. Gurcharan knew this was the very least of his concerns, and tough conversations lay ahead.

Over the next few days Gurcharan broke the news about the proposed move to England. The conversation was much more awkward this time around, and he needed his sister more than ever to help convince them all. After much deliberation his mind was made up, and he knew managing expectations with family and Charanjit wasn't going to be easy.

Swarn Kaur didn't let Gurcharan down and was instrumental in persuading the rest of the family, especially their father. She pointed out that in the time Inder had been working abroad, his contribution had helped greatly. Gurcharan would be under the guidance of his brother, and they would be able to support each other.

Surjan Singh was left at a crossroad as to what to do. The risk of letting another son go to a foreign land could create a divide within the family. Life had taught him that no matter how firm the bond, distance could impact on relationships. However, he was mindful that with Gurcharan in England, Inder would no longer be alone.

Where he'd so reluctantly let one son go, how could he stop another? Therefore, with great reservation he gave Gurcharan his blessings, but warned him that the ultimate decision on whether he went or not rested with Charanjit. They were both engaged to each other, and he no longer had the power in making decisions without her input. This union now meant they had a duty of care towards each other.

A prized asset no more

The fifteen-hour drive from Tehran to Herat in Afghanistan meant a change of guard at the steering wheel every couple of hours. Tejinder had mentioned there was a petrol station just before the border crossing, and strongly recommended they fill up before driving any further.

Fuel for the body was also essential and there was no shortage of that now. Their hosts had been kind enough to pack them a box full of fruit, veg and non-veg traditional curry, and with romali roti's stacked high. There was also a small tub of baklava which provided a much-needed sugar boost when required. The fragrance of the food floated throughout the car, with everyone licking their fingers in appreciation each time.

Winding roads lined their path, and the silhouette of the mountains stood still against the false light of the moon. The scene unfolding in front of them created a tranquil beauty that was well admired by anyone who was still awake. Driving had to be extra careful as there was no telling what was around the bend, and each time the bright moon hid behind one of the mountains they were engulfed in total darkness.

It was 5:00am when they reached the border crossing. While one of the officers inspected their paperwork, the other couldn't stop noticing the persistent yawning by everyone. He advised them to stop over and rest, and they appreciated the advice.

As the sun began to rise it revealed the barren land which now lined the road they were travelling on. Surprisingly, the quality of the roads wasn't anything like they'd expected. In fact, the road was like a solid white slab, stretching for miles. The thick groove between the slabs made a small thumping noise each time they drove over it, ensuring the passengers dazed in and out of sleep.

Over the horizon a sea of camels started appearing either side. Inder slowed down and carefully manoeuvred around them, with the sound of the car automatically driving them into a frenzy. To be on the safe side, each time their car approached a group of camels, Inder pressed the horn to give them enough time to disperse.

The brothers were very tired and had to remain extra vigilant, but they couldn't hide the constant yawning. This was enough to encourage Roy to put his hat in the ring and take control of the wheel. He insisted on driving as being a spectator for so long tipped him over the edge.

Inder was hesitant at first as he was aware Roy's eyesight wasn't the best. However, after much consideration, and the fact that it was a straight road, the risk seemed minimal. His only instruction was to drive slowly and be alert at pressing the horn.

With a bumpy start Roy soon found rhythm, with his knuckles turning white as he gripped the steering wheel. Hunched forward with his eyes focusing with all their might, he peered through those thick frames, driving slowly and straight as possible. Further ahead another herd of camels roamed on the horizon. Just as before when the car veered closer, they started parting to walk in the other direction. Roy was convinced it was their natural reaction and so ignored the need to beep the horn.

With the sun shining ever so brightly, one of the camels opted not to run in the opposite direction. Instead, it headed straight towards their car and collided with the bonnet, propelling itself straight over the top. The whole incident happened in a flash and the noise was like a crash of thunder. The camel landed on his stomach with a thud so loud that it reverberated throughout the car.

Roy pressed the brake hard, making a screeching noise and bringing the car to a halt. Sarita peered from the back window at the camel who was now laying very still. Burying Kunal's head into her lap, she hoped the camel would make some movement. But that hope faded with each passing moment and they were all disappointed and filled with sadness.

The sound of the running engine had been drowned out by gasps and sobbing. Roy's head was slumped onto the steering wheel, he wished the ground had opened up and swallowed him. Inder took control of his senses and checked that everyone was ok. Then he contemplated getting out of the car and checking the camel. The initial noise had frightened the other camels away however, some had started congregating nearby.

On the verge of opening the door Inder stopped as Roy started to babble something to him. Regaining his composure, he looked Inder straight in the eyes and warned him of danger they could all find themselves in if they remained here any longer. A camel was regarded as a very important asset to the people of Afghanistan. This was their livelihood and now a group of foreigners had just deprived someone of their prized possession and future income.

Luckily, there was no ranting camel owner in sight, but Roy knew they didn't have much time. Gurcharan scrambled out of the car to discover the bonnet was damaged quite badly however, in the grand scheme of things they had been very lucky not to have picked up any physical injuries. Ushering Roy to the back seat,

Gurcharan took charge of the steering wheel and they sped off leaving only a trail of dust behind them.

The Austin Cambridge couldn't have eaten up the road any faster! No doubt they'd have broken any previous speed records that existed to date by pushing this car to its limit. Having driven for some miles they came to a standstill at the next village. Small single storey brick houses were wedged together, some with no windows or doors. Behind the houses a large patch of dry land provided the ideal opportunity to drive into and remain undetected.

Since leaving the fatal incident with the camel, they had only one thing on their mind, and that was to wash the blood off the car. Sarita kept Kunal in the car, he was visibly shaken by the loud thud the camel had caused. Thankfully he hadn't seen the camel sprawled across the road behind them.

Wiping the blood stains off the car was not an easy task. It had quickly dried against the heat. Gurcharan scrubbed hard with one of the stockings and some water from a bottle. Once the blood had been wiped off, they left the small quiet village, constantly looking in the back window from fear of being spotted or being followed. Such an offence would certainly mean facing an angry mob of locals seeking some sort of revenge.

They travelled a further thirty miles before deciding to stop and get some rest. It had been two hours since the border crossing and Herat was now in their line of vision. Conscious of being caught by the owner of the dead camel, they parked behind two pyramid shaped lumps of rubble. The image of the camel was still very fresh in their minds, with the loud thud still ringing in Inder and Gurcharan's ears. All the passengers shut their eyes and tried to bring some peace within themselves.

Sometime later, Kunal woke up by a rare noise of a car zooming by. He went to wake up his mother, who in turn nudged Roy, and he tapped the brothers. With a degree of caution, the brothers stepped out to conduct a more in-depth inspection of the car. Once again it needed urgent repairs. No doubt, in its current state it would attract unwanted attention from the local people.

News of the dead camel would have travelled like wildfire, and they could be on Afghanistan's most wanted list.

On finally reaching Herat, they managed to locate a small garage with the help of a tea stall owner. Luckily the garage owner accepted the car without asking too many questions and pointed them to nearby accommodation. That evening everyone was still on edge, and a nervous feeling loomed in the air. Roy was panicking, and almost certain that word had spread and somehow, they were all wanted for a hideous crime.

This led to a restless night's sleep. Inder and Gurcharan were now close to home, but they felt the most vulnerable during this journey. Accepting some things were out of their control, it helped dispel some of the feeling of sadness. With that positive thinking, they embraced each other and congratulated themselves for having survived some seventeen days on the road. Their destination was within reach.

An eerie silence loomed outside, and Inder woke suddenly as if consumed by a nightmare of sorts. It was quiet, Gurcharan was still sleeping. This was a positive sign, as the silence meant no one had come looking for them. There had been no angry mob of people, or herds of camels looking to put them to the sword. Regardless, the intention was not to prolong their stay in Herat, and as soon as everyone was awake and ready, Inder was keen to get back on the road and drive to Kabul.

The birds barely had a chance to open their beaks and signal the arrival of the new day that they were back on the road. Beyond their simple accommodation, Herat was a bustling city with wide roads, and buses with no windows beeping their way past cars, sharing what space was left with people and animal traffic.

There were signs of development here too. Steel structures stood tall against the blue sky with piles of brickwork left on the road just in front. Good road signs made navigating easy, seeing they had some 800km of driving to negotiate before reaching Kabul.

1964 - Held by a thin thread

In the weeks that followed their engagement, talk of fixing a wedding date was already underway. In between it all Gurcharan and Charanjit continued to meet when possible, but those meetings were about to take a new turn.

Gurcharan was not himself as he waited for Charanjit. It was a lunch date but one Gurcharan could have delayed. The conversation flowed one way as they sat at the local restaurant waiting for their food to arrive. Charanjit sensed something was not right and queried Gurcharan.

After a pause and puff of the cheeks, Gurcharan slid his hands onto Charanjit's and began to unravel his predicament. He began setting the scene, talking about how well Inder was now doing in England. But with that he also talked about the feeling of loneliness Inder was experiencing. For that reason, Inder asked for Gurcharan to join him.

Charanjit's first reaction was of sympathy, encouraging her fiancé that he should visit his brother. But Gurcharan hadn't mentioned the phrase ***visit***. Maybe he hadn't conveyed the message clearly as Charanjit went on to recommend a few weeks in England wouldn't do any harm. If that was the sole reason for his glum demeanour then this would solve the problem in her estimation.

Looking back at her with watery eyes, and loving her innocence, he delivered the news. That it wasn't a visit for a couple of weeks but, the possibly of staying in England for up to two years. As if the floor had been moved from under her feet, the look of encouragement and innocence was now replaced with confusion and worry.

Trying to grasp the words uttered by Gurcharan, she asked him to repeat what he had just said, and then broke down in tears. The tea was still in the cups as the young boy picked up the plates off the wooden table, its inhabitants had now long gone.

Later that evening, Mr Nanda visited the Chhatwal household, and a serious discussion took place with Surjan Singh and Gurcharan. Mr Nanda's concern was for the welfare of his daughter. Not able to conceal his emotions he directed his concerns at Surjan Singh and that such a gap between engagement *and marriage risked their very future. He voiced concerns of single men living abroad and then adopting western ideals.*

Surjan Singh was asked to provide assurances, guaranteeing that Gurcharan would remain interested in making Charanjit his life partner. Gurcharan interjected, assuring his future father in law that he loved Charanjit, and that their relationship was stronger than he thought. With nothing more to add, Mr Nanda requested leave, stating that the survival of the relationship now depended on Gurcharan and Charanjit themselves.

Over the next few weeks meetings between the two felt strained. The mood was sombre with Charanjit probing Gurcharan on whether he would change his mind about going. The future of their relationship, according to her was now held together by a thin thread.

Like before, Gurcharan maintained his stance that the visit would be for no more than two years, and that in between that time he would make provisions to come back and see her. Initially Gurcharan had not been keen on the idea of going to England to work. He had a very good job in India, was close to his family and then there was Charanjit.

But the need to be with his brother at this moment was greater. While his father slept comfortably in the notion that Inder was working as hard as he could, he was unaware of what loneliness could do. Even a house full of other immigrants could feel lonely on occasions.

1965 – Mind made up

It was an exceptionally hot day in July as Gurcharan sat at the restaurant table staring at Charanjit. He was flying off to England in under three weeks, and this was to be the last time they'd have lunch together. Whatever was to happen would happen, it now remained in the **hands of God***, her final words as they parted.*

She knew that an engagement lasting two years was near impossible, and on top of that they'd be the talk of the town. In her heart she couldn't dispel the thought that Gurcharan would be living and working amongst white women who, with their education and beauty had more to offer then herself. Their white skin would be too much for anyone to resist, and that in this period her beloved fiancé would be consumed by British culture.

Charanjit was neither hasty nor brave enough to call off the relationship and would rather let things linger on in his absence. In the days that followed their last meeting, Gurcharan remained quiet. He asked himself whether England was worth putting his personal future on hold. Furthermore, risking it to end before it even got started?

As the plane ascended from Delhi International Airport, carrying another member of the Chhatwal family, Gurcharan was in deep thought about what he was leaving behind. There were several relationships back home which hopefully, could cope with his absence for the short term. Sadly, he didn't feel the same level of confidence for his personal relationship, and such situations rarely survived the distance.

Austin, we must depart

Crossing into Kabul, the passengers instantly noticed the bustling nature of the city. Men were dressed in a traditional Salwar Kameez[14], with long coats and colourful turbans. People moved in all directions as traffic weaved around them or waited patiently until it was safe to do so. In Iran, Tejinder had mentioned how Afghanistan was trying to adopt some western ideals while conforming to traditions.

They witnessed some of that in Herat however, Kabul was a step back in time. The roads were uneven and in need of much attention. Evidence of this was the large truck in front of them swaying from side to side and struggling to maintain balance. Unsure of which direction they were supposed to be heading, Gurcharan noticed some Sardars[15] co-habiting at a tea

---

[14] The outfit consists of a knee length dress and baggy trousers
[15] The term Sardars originated from Persia and refers to 'commander'. However, it is also reference to a Sikh who wears a turban and maintains a beard.

stall, and took a moment to speak to them. Instantly they made Gurcharan feel very welcome and were overjoyed to hear of how long they had been on the road. Gurcharan explained that their intention was to stay in Kabul for around two days, and so the Sardars took it upon themselves to help with securing suitable accommodation.

Later that evening, the same group of Sardars met up with them all for a tour of the local market. Occupying a large piece of land, the market was like a maze full of traders selling all sorts of delights. From fresh meat to dried fruit, to items of clothing such as shawls and shoes. These stalls barely had space for more than one person, yet somehow squeezed generations of owners beside each other to assist customers. To watch them in action was truly satisfying, with each one drawing on an array of expertise.

Navigating to a stall that was owned by one of the Sardars, they found them to be hard working and diligent people. These Sardars were also living in a foreign country while applying their trade, a trait all too familiar with the Chhatwal brothers. But what stood out was the level of hospitality that was shown. Having only been acquainted some hours ago, it felt like they had known each other for a long time. Words were softly spoken, and with a tone that oozed a humble nature. Eyes twinkled with happiness and smiles beamed from one ear to another.

Inder was overwhelmed by this show of love and respect. Turning to Gurcharan, he said their parents would have described these people as **soft like butter and sweet like sugar**. They found the Sardar traders genuinely affectionate. This was in no way a ploy to increase potential sales. If there was one single skill the Chhatwal brothers had learned during this trip, that was in the art of understanding body language and a person's intentions.

So much had happened since they left Slough a couple of weeks ago. The incident in Yugoslavia with the local Police was probably the turning point, it was a close encounter and seemed to have set the tone for a difficult and often challenging journey from that moment. Their biggest fear had moved from potential issues with the car to getting lost or coming across local groups in an unknown land and being at the end of some hideous treatment.

All that was forgotten, and the evening was one of relaxation and reflection, each sharing their road experience with newfound friends. Inder even came up with a collective name, the **Sardars of Kabul**. In such a short space of time the affection had turned to one of wellbeing and safety, and for this reason the Sardars advised them not to travel through Pakistan. Taking the risk to travel without a valid visa would have all sorts of permutations. This could result in all of them being arrested, and even put into jail.

Inder and Gurcharan were aware that the political situation in Pakistan and its relationship with India was exceptionally delicate. Just two years prior both countries had been engaged in military action against each other. Jammu and Kashmir were at the heart of the problem as Pakistan launched *Operation Gibraltar* to infiltrate Indian forces. India had retaliated by attacking West Pakistan, resulting in a seventeen-day war between the two and resulting in many casualties.

Eventually it took the intervention of the United Nations to call a ceasefire and bring the war to an end. Wounds were still fresh in the minds of people on both sides! Therefore, arriving unannounced, with a car full of passengers from non-Pakistani heritage, would be like placing your head into the mouth of a hungry lion.

A deep discussion took place and after much deliberation, it was suggested they fly from Kabul to India. During the long exchange, no one spoke about the Austin Cambridge. Without saying it, Inder and Gurcharan knew exactly what the car's eventual fate would be. Roy started talking about transport options but Sarita interrupted, and then gently told him to forget about making provisions for it.

Roy was visibly distraught. However, he understood the logic and succumbed to the bigger picture. They all agreed to purchase tickets the next day and take the next available flight to Amritsar with Ariana Airlines.

The resolute Austin Morris Cambridge Estate, the car that bore the bruises of their journey, a place they called home for the past few weeks, and the car that didn't once suffer a puncture, would be left in Kabul for now. Whether it would be collected was not a decision for today, but Roy hoped to address it as soon they landed in India. For now, the burning urge he had been carrying inside for so long began to diminish.

Sarita, not wanting to totally deflate her husband's feelings, consoled him and reminded him that it was their collective achievements in England that would prove their families wrong, and not the car. It was, no doubt, a hard pill to swallow.

Later that evening, provisions were made for the safe keeping of the car. It was parked in a small warehouse belonging to one of the traders. All the contents in the boot and dashboard were emptied and any mess inside swept up. The remaining tins of food and stockings were left with the trader offering up the space. Before shutting the large wooden doors, Inder and Gurcharan sat in the car one last time, playing out each scene repeatedly as they passed through the countries.

This British built car was designed for the flat roads of England, but remarkably had withstood all types of terrain and physical damage. In that moment, the brothers joked that if they ever had the chance to speak to the people behind this fine car, that they would shake their hands and tell them this beautiful machine did them proud.

Before retiring to bed, Inder and Gurcharan mentioned to the Sardars of their intention to visit Harmandir Sahib, the holiest place of worship for Sikhs. In their final goodbyes, the Sardars made a special request. Each of them handed over the vast sum of five hundred Rupees. They humbly asked the brothers to partake in Ardas (Sikh prayer) on their behalf, for well-being, courage and continuation of faith.

These were God-fearing Sikhs who despite living in another country, maintained strong emotional connections back home. The brothers were honoured to be entrusted with this responsibility and assured them their donations and prayers would be delivered.

1965 - Now there were two

Gurcharan arrived in England on 25th July 1965. He was greeted at the airport by around thirty people, whereas two years ago it was only Inder. A truly momentous occasion, and for the first time Inder had a blood relation in this new land. Gurcharan made his way towards the arrivals bay while walking slowly and taking in the moment. He'd heard a lot about England from Inder, but the realisation that he was here was stirring mixed emotions in him.

On entering through the white double doors and into the arrivals section, he instantly spotted Inder. It was an embrace that lasted a lifetime, with both having not seen each other for so long. Gurcharan was taken aback by the number of people that had come to receive him. Inder wanted to make sure there was no lonely ride in a taxi this time around.

The warm sun of a Sunday afternoon greeted the brothers as they both walked out of Heathrow Airport. Pulling out of the car park, they were followed by a convoy of cars, and it felt like a celebrity had just arrived. Gurcharan realised his brother had accomplished a good standing amongst friends who were very much strangers to each other two years ago.

En-route they first headed to a local Gurdwara as Inder had arranged a Langer De Seva[16] service. The strong traditions that the brothers had instilled in them were still firmly present. As important as it was to take blessings at Harmandir Sahib before leaving for England, it was equally important to take blessings on the safe arrival of Gurcharan. The Langer De Seva symbolised the sharing of their happiness amongst the congregation, and a way of saying thanks to God.

Gurdwara Shepherd Bush was located on Sinclair Road in Putney[17], South London. Although it was a house used for worship, the feel and ambience were much the same. Upon entering, there was a sense of peace and tranquillity that flowed through this Holy establishment. Inder and some friends had

---

[16] Langer is referred to as "free kitchen" in Sikhism where food is served to anyone from any background or faith; it is provided by the Gurdwara. Any member of the congregation is therefore allowed to contribute either via a financial or food donation towards that food as goodwill and a blessing.

[17] The congregation remained at this location until 1969, at which point they moved to a building known as Norland Castle, Queensdale Road, London. To this day the Gurdwara remains central to the local and far reaching community.

made a financial donation to the Gurdwara as part of the service, and this would be used for day to day supplies for the wider congregation. With respects paid and blessings obtained, the Chhatwal brothers headed to Gurcharan's new home, a place Inder had made his own.

Ahead of his trip, Gurcharan had been advised by Inder not to be too surprised about the accommodation he was going to live in. It was small, felt cramped and he would miss the open space of the veranda back home. Gurcharan was wise not to raise his level of expectation, as for now it was all about settling in as quick as possible. Like his brother before him, the key was finding potential work, and with it taking his mind off the heartache of leaving Charanjit in India.

Upon arrival at the house Gurcharan was welcomed by the landlords who spoke highly of Inder. It was not common to have Indian landlords in England, so the occupants of this house had been fortunate. They treated everyone fairly and with respect, which was a world away from some of the experiences elsewhere often talked about.

That evening Gurcharan ate very little because of the hearty meal at the Gurdwara and with time zones playing havoc.

Sharing a room with his brother, Inder listened attentively to Gurcharan about his current situation with Charanjit. As his brother spoke in a low tone, Inder felt some sadness and guilt.

It seems the timing hadn't been ideal, but he consoled Gurcharan that the sooner he steadied himself things would improve back home. Inside Inder was praying for patience for his brother and Charanjit, but he himself had no control over the matter.

The Motherland is on the horizon

The taxi ride to Kabul airport took around an hour. It was bumpy and not as comfortable as the Austin Cambridge. Such was the connection to the car that it was hard to think if any other would come as close for affection. Roy was quiet and battling with mixed emotions. For the brothers, it was the first time in twenty days that they didn't have to worry about directions and destinations.

There wasn't the burden of having to navigate their way through unknown towns and narrow streets. Now they were able to peer out of the back window of a car, to see the vast lands for what they were, as opposed to an endless road. Yet at the same time they missed the element of control and responsibility they were given, without doubt there was a certain pride in that.

Kabul International Airport was a mass of concrete built by the Russians. It was very small in comparison to Heathrow Airport, or even Delhi Airport. However, all they wanted to do was get on their flight and go home. With luggage checked in, the waiting time seemed to drag on, and the anticipation of finally getting home was creating an overwhelming feeling in their hearts.

The patience everyone had shown for so long was being peeled back like old wallpaper to reveal an emotional state. Slowly, two groups formed and the passengers who were together for so long, cramped in a restricted space were now creating space between each other.

Inder and Gurcharan's minds were only settled once they sat firmly in their seats. Experiencing the jittering of the plane as it took off, they left Kabul and were now flying high above the land and buildings which looked like small dots. As the outside winds battled against the metal frame of the plane, inside, each member of the road trip (except Kunal who was sound asleep) battled with their own emotions.

Roy was still downbeat about leaving his beloved car behind and deep down he knew that he may never see it again. Sarita was nervous about meeting her family after so many years, not knowing whether the reunion would be one of forgiveness or further stubbornness.

As for Inder and Gurcharan, they were thankful to be finally heading home in one piece. Forever grateful for the experience, each marvelled at the driving and miles they had covered. But they were slightly disappointed not to have made that final drive through Pakistan, to the doorstep of India. The brothers scoffed the food handed over by the stewardess in record time. They tried hard to stay awake, but burning eyes were fighting against them and eventually the battle was won, and total darkness prevailed.

Having been nudged by a staff member to wake up, Gurcharan and Inder had missed the message from the pilot advising passengers to fasten their seat belts. Very soon, the plane would be making its descent with rubber bouncing against the runway. The brothers clutched their rather unusual looking overcoats tightly in their hands, it seems they were nervous about something. Inder looked in the direction of Gurcharan and questioned whether bringing these bulky coats was such a good idea after all.

This new episode occurred when they were in Kabul and involved the daughter of the hotel owner. She had advised the brothers that instead of carrying heavy sweaters in their luggage, they'd be better suited to hold them in their hands. This way they wouldn't run the risk of being charged for too much weight. Inder was unsure about this, and almost certain airport authorities would push back on the carrying of multiple items. Then she had an idea! Opening the stitching on the coats, she hid the sweaters inside.

Being naive, they took her words as gospel when she explained this was indeed common practice. Both had felt uneasy about it but didn't push back in the likely event of upsetting the young lady.

As the plane touched down onto the tarmac the brothers sighed with relief and emotion. Large tears welled up in their eyes as they patted each other on the back. Moments later the fear and trepidation kicked in as they made their way to the security desk.

All necessary passport and security checks went well, until they were about to leave the customs section. Gurcharan felt a hand on his shoulder, the uniformed official pointed to the bottom of his coat. There, dangling from the side was an arm of a thick knitted sweater. It seemed the stitching had given way on the coat from the sheer weight of the sweaters. They were moved to one side for further inspection, and the brothers panicked. However, the uniformed official was a fair man, and on hearing their story of the road trip handed out just a verbal warning. But nonetheless he was amazed at the journey they had made and hugged them both very tightly and bid them farewell quickly as he could see they were eager to meet their families.

The time had come for them all to part their separate ways and take the next steps in their journey. Inder and Gurcharan thanked Roy and his family for giving them this opportunity and entrusting them to safely transport his family.

Their parting was totally opposite to the emotions they all shared during the road trip. Roy was cold and there were no hugs exchanged; it almost felt like the employer was relieving his employees. Just a handshake and pat on the back was the gesture of thanks. Roy didn't even offer details of his place of residence nor did he show any desire to meet when they got back to England. This left Inder and Gurcharan with a twinge of disappointment as they had hoped for a different outcome on reaching India.

1965 – Blue envelope

A few weeks had passed, and Charanjit was up early to begin her weekend chores around the house. Her preference was to tackle housework first thing, and therefore allowing the rest of the day to her own thoughts.

With a warm day in prospect, she made washing and the drying of clothes her first course of action. Each item of clothing was soaked in a bucket of warm water, plucked out and carefully smothered in soap. Then with vigorous force, two fists pumped their way through the clothing to ensure the soap was swished everywhere. Once the punching was complete, Charanjit dipped the clothing back into the water and pressed it down. The final task involved slamming the clothes against a concrete slab before hanging it out to dry.

Charanjit completed her chores in diligent fashion and trotted to her bedroom for a short break when she noticed a blue envelope sitting on her dressing table. Aside from her exam results she'd never had any other post addressed to her name. The style and colour told her it was from outside of India.

Carefully opening the letter, and seeing her name at the top, her heart began to melt to the very words written by Gurcharan. He spoke of his initial thoughts of England and of the people who shared the same accommodation. He asked of her family, and then of her wellbeing.

The letter was brief and with that he wished her well in the hope he would see a letter in return, only if she felt it was the right thing to do. She hoped he had written more, he felt distant, but her disappointment soon changed to relief that he did take the time to write. He hadn't forgotten her altogether yet.

1966 – Gurcharan finds his feet

Nothing much had changed at the residence where Inder and Gurcharan were living. A few months after Gurcharan's arrival Chanan Singh had gone back to India to get married. Now he was back, accompanied by his wife who moved in with him. They both had their own room and strict guidelines were observed in terms of separation of the new lady and other inhabitants.

During early periods of settling in Gurcharan drew on some good observations. All those in the house had a firm bond with each other, they looked after one another, and shared in cooking and cleaning. Tasty food could be smelt throughout the house most of the day as occupants arrived and left in accordance to their work patterns.

Like his brother Inder, Gurcharan also placed great emphasis on his appearance. His beard remained uncut; his hair long and covered by his turban. Inder had told Gurcharan of the time when he was advised to cut his hair and how Chanan Singh stood by his decision when he refused.

Over the coming weeks Gurcharan carefully observed a further change in the mood of Chanan Singh. He was no longer cutting his beard and later started wearing a turban. Both the brothers congratulated him on this decision and at the same time dismissed any praise directed back at them for being the sole reason for this change.

Once Gurcharan was settled, Chanan Singh again took the role of transporting him around different places of work to find a job. His background was that of a mechanical engineer however, nothing as such was on offer. Having read about a job based in Windsor for an engineer, Gurcharan decided to attend the interview. He was the first turbaned Sikh to set foot in that establishment, and it was fair to say they had never seen anyone of his appearance before.

The company was called Fred Mayer and the interviewer was a man named Jim Mathews. A man of gentle nature he quickly warmed to Gurcharan. However, unsure about the pay and standard of work, Gurcharan left his details but didn't pursue it any further. A few days later there was a knock on the door, and it was Jim Mathews who had come to offer the job.

Over the coming months, Gurcharan made good strides in the company and struck up a strong working relationship with Jim. Whenever there was an opportunity for any overtime, he would first offer it to Gurcharan. This was an ideal scenario when one was single and looking to build up some money.

There were also free education classes on offer in the local area, and with Gurcharan being from a professional background, he took full advantage. But to attend these courses required strong organisational skills with regards to prioritising work and home life. A typical day would entail finishing work to ensure he caught the bus in time to reach Windsor for 7:00pm.

From there, he would take a brisk walk lasting some twenty minutes to the college to study his City & Guilds Diploma. The course finished at 9:00pm and to save money he would walk the forty-minute journey home. On the odd occasion when there were no leftovers, he would apply himself in the kitchen and cook.

One morning, Gurcharan was getting ready for work when Chanan Singh shouted from the bottom of the stairs to inform him he had post. Excited, he ran downstairs like a child who had just got a new toy and plucked the envelope from Chanan Singh's hand. The sender's address on the back instantly warmed up his heart. Charanjit had written back, and he wasn't leaving the house until he read what was written.

Walking into the kitchen he sat himself down and opened the letter. The first line read **my dearest Gurcharan**. *He pushed the letter close to his chest, there was no one here, and he continued to read on. Charanjit thanked him for his letter, and she spoke of how overwhelmed and pleased she was to hear from him. She was glad he was settling in well and asked him what the people were like, whether he had made any friends, and how work was.*

Gurcharan read the letter a few more times before tucking it inside his jacket pocket, then he got up and made his way to the front door. Informing Inder he was about to leave; his eyes were full of water but there was joy in them. The letters, he hoped, would help protect that thin thread they both spoke of, and all it needed was commitment in keeping contact.

In the year that followed Gurcharan's arrival, a total of ten letters had crossed oceans back and forth with the aim of keeping this long-distance relationship alive. No sooner would Gurcharan finish posting a letter that he would start thinking about what to write in the next. This spurred him on to find new things to do, so that he had more interesting facts to write about. Every letter he wrote included a reminder to Charanjit that work, along with being with his brother was the main reason he was in England.

Charanjit's latest letter posed the question which Gurcharan was hoping to avoid at all costs. When would he be coming back? Charanjit's mood once again dropped when she read that Gurcharan would not be coming back any time soon. Citing cost and work constraints as a valid reason, he requested that Charanjit remain patient. That they would be together very soon.

The turn of the year signalled almost eighteen months since Gurcharan and Charanjit's engagement. They had never envisaged being in this situation when they took the first step towards a concrete future. But now Charanjit hadn't written back for a couple of months. She was normally very quick in responding but he knew the reason why she had not written back to him.

Gurcharan decided not to push the issue and let things progress as they were, he would write no more letters now. He humbly requested from his sister that she deliver a message in person to Charanjit, that he loved her and hoped she would wait for his arrival back home.

1966 – Time for a new home

This was a significant time in England's history and with it the brothers too. On that historic Saturday at Wembley, the England football team defeated their rivals West Germany 4-2 to win the world cup. The country had gone mad with joy, with Inder and Gurcharan glad to have witnessed it on tv.

While the Wembley turf became home to these world cup winning heroes, it was time for others to leave for a new home. The dynamics in the house had changed since the arrival of Chanan Singh's wife. While space and privacy were well observed, it didn't feel quite the same.

It was now time that Inder and Gurcharan took Chanan Singh's blessings and stood on their own two feet. Just a few weeks after England won the world cup, the brothers moved out, renting a house just a few streets away on Petersfield Avenue. It felt strange at first, now without the noise of other house mates, but they soon became accustomed to having the independence of their own living space.

However, it did mean more effort was needed to keep the house clean. The brothers kept in contact with their previous house mates and would regularly invite them over for dinner and a catch up.

1967 – Where did the time go since landing?

It was the turn of the year and now Surjan Singh Chhatwal had two sons making positive headway in England. They had worked hard to dispel his initial fears and frequently kept contact with the family. While it never felt the same, regular dialog was essential to preserve relationships. In their letters home, they often mentioned how welcoming the people of this new land were, and how there were lots of opportunities for work and to make money.

They spoke of the good standard of living, the beautiful houses with their neat gardens. However, there were certain elements of their early experiences they were not willing to share. Like the cramped accommodation they had lived in, and the fact that on some days it felt like a challenge to uphold their appearance and beliefs.

The brothers were never the target of direct racism however, experienced subtle brushes with regards to feeling outcast amongst their white co-workers. Not drinking alcohol when with Indian co-workers at the local pub made them the centre of jokes. There had been countless occasions where the brothers had to remind colleagues that cutting hair and shaving the beard was not necessary in obtaining success. Inder and Gurcharan were living proof that not compromising on your Sikh identity was something others admired as opposed to frown upon.

In work they gained the respect of their peers and management however, also sensed some frustration from the local English people looking on as jobs were being taken by immigrants.

England was also a place not immune from the disease of poverty. Homeless men and women perched on street corners begging for money, certainly not the outlook of a country that promised financial progress. They'd often spot adverts in newspapers from landlords which clearly stated, **no dogs, no blacks, no Irish**.

Inder and Gurcharan never directly experienced taunts or turban related issues, but they'd heard stories that filled them with sadness. Notably an incident that was brewing in Wolverhampton, further North of England. A fellow Indian man by the name of Tarsem Singh Sandhu had been suspended from his job as a bus conductor after wearing a turban and keeping a beard.

Gurcharan had read in the newspaper that company regulations stipulated coming to work clean shaven and wearing a cap. Mr Tarsem's refusal to back down from removing his beard and turban had cost him his job. Some 6,000 Sikhs marched to the local town hall in protest, with around 50,000 marching in Delhi. Mr Sandhu was being supported by the UK president of the Shiromani Akali Dal, Mr Sohan Singh Jolly. How this was going to transpire they had no idea.

While they were sympathetic to the cause and hoped this matter would end peacefully, like many others they kept their heads down and worked. They had promised their family a return in five years. Yet there was a voice inside telling them to see loved ones sooner. Just as they had declined to share some of their more intimate fears, Inder and Gurcharan were certain their loved ones were also holding back on emotions.

One road trip ends, another journey begins

The walk from passport control to the entrance was short however, the brothers' feet felt heavy. Excitement and emotions swelled up inside, and they were fighting against an army of butterflies moving around in their stomachs. With each step their hearts pounded through their chests at the thought of that embrace. Both were convinced their family would show unconditional love on seeing them. Hope rested on the fact this joy would overshadow the worries each family member would have endured over the past so many weeks.

The warm October air gently pushed against their faces as they walked out. The city of Amritsar was bustling with the noise of people and traffic, and the smells of food floated straight up their nostrils. This was home and it was the best place in the world. None of the countries they passed through could compare to that feeling.

The romantic trance was broken by the ever-increasing sound of voices and footsteps and it was then that they spotted their family. Inder and Gurcharan bent down to touch their parent's feet and remained there for what seemed like an age. It wasn't to do with the fear of being told off but rather the blessing and assurance they needed.

Their father kept running his hands across both their turbans and beards, with pride and happiness in his eyes. This was his biggest relief, that his sons were still intact with their appearance. Everyone was overwhelmed in that moment, with tears of joy flowing down cheeks as their mother hugged them continuously. Joined by extended family, their arrival was celebrated with garlands of flowers.

On leaving the airport, the first stop was Harmandir Sahib to pay their respects. They wanted to thank God for protecting them throughout their journey, and not just on the road trip. Also, they had made a promise to the Sardars of Kabul to pass on their prayers.

The visit to Harmandir Sahib offered them the chance to take solace in what they had achieved. Many times Inder and Gurcharan had reflected on their adventure, each time they drove into a country, and with each person they encountered. Now, amongst the community they recognised and knew so well, a humble pride gripped their body. If only they could inform the Sardars of Kabul that their prayers had been offered. However, deep inside there was a feeling these hard working and God-fearing people would continue to enjoy success.

It was time to head back to the town they left a long time ago, Hoshiarpur. Surjan Singh mentioned the family had opened an Akhand Path[18] for Inder and Gurcharan's arrival. When Gurcharan walked through the door he was greeted by his prospective in-laws, and suddenly, he felt he had reached the very peak of all these celebrations. It felt like he had conquered the highest mountain. What felt like a dire situation with Charanjit, with both so far away was now a memory he

---

[18] Akhand Path is the common practise of continuous recitation (without any break) of sacred religious texts in Sikhism.

simply threw away. The thin thread was not so thin after all.

Charanjit's parents brought with them sagan[19] as confirmation that he was now a member of their family too. For Gurcharan, while one journey came to an end, he was now firmly embarking on another.

All those present joined in prayers which were followed by home cooked vegetarian food. After the ceremonies were finished, Inder and Gurcharan recounted their experiences in England and on the road to a waiting audience. Young members listened attentively as the brothers re-told each episode in detail, often talking about Roy, Sarita and Kunal who kept them going on this long drive. Every so often, the mention of a bad experience would bring a gasp from their parents followed by a thankful blessing, and it felt as if they were right there with them in that moment.

---

[19] Sagan is a ceremony where two families exchange gifts and sweets by way of confirmation of their children entering into marriage.

As the evening grew closer Gurcharan and Inder took leave of the family to get some well-earned rest. Not much had changed at the house, with their bedrooms looking just as they left them a few years ago. Their bed may have been hard as a rock compared to the one in England, but it brought instant assurance and comfort.

It was fair to say the brothers, along with the other house mates never got too climatised with the beds in England. They would love to have slept in, but more time was spent working then resting. Like so many other immigrants across England, Inder and Gurcharan took every opportunity that came their way to work more hours and earn as much money as possible.

Not going to sleep straight away the dark night presented a moment of reflection. Inder thought back to that bold decision to jump out of the taxi and connect with a total stranger. Gurcharan on leaving his relationship in the balance to provide much needed support for his brother.

Then to travel with a family they had never met before, and to drive through all those countries and experience the highs and lows that unfolded before them. Their journey back home came with ensuring the safety of a family whose reasons for travelling still left them unsure right to the end. Savouring their first night back, it wasn't long before a deep trance took over as their heads rested onto the pillows.

Everyone had expected Gurcharan and Inder to sleep in however, to their surprise both the brothers were up bright and early. Like excited children, they didn't want to waste a moment in absorbing morning sunlight, or the smells and sounds of their home city. Those sounds and smells hadn't changed and while this was a positive thing, they were disappointed that their living conditions had remained unchanged.

The rented accommodation was much the same, only that it had aged even more and in need of urgent improvements. A large proportion of their weekly salary in England was sent back home without delay, and they never stipulated how the money was to be used. What was important that it provided the necessary support for daily needs and future commitments.

Inder and Gurcharan left India with the purpose of making a better life not just for themselves but also for their extended family. However, they felt progression had not reached the level they had expected.

Now the desire to move the family away from rented accommodation burned bright and hard within them. They wanted their parents to be proud owners of their own home. With limited time it was critical they took every opportunity available to turn this dream into a reality.

We're here, so time for change

A week had passed since the end of the road trip and plans were made to visit extended family in Chandigarh. Gurcharan travelled alone as he didn't want to burden the family with too many visitors.

Chandigarh was renowned for its modern outlook and cleanliness, and with a bustling town centre. Walking from shop to shop, Gurcharan recognised a familiar face perched outside a cinema. The large lettering above the man's head read *Kiran*. In front of the man was a small table stacked with folders. As Gurcharan edged closer, he realised that the man sitting quietly on the chair was none other than his old school friend, Om Prakash.

Gurcharan couldn't believe his luck at meeting his friend, and a chance meeting was an excellent opportunity to catch up over a cup of tea. Om Prakash ushered over the boy standing near the box office to bring some tea and snacks. They both exchanged memories of old, laughed over silly school pranks and consoled each other at friends who were no more.

On the subject of work, it transpired that Om had just started a new business in real estate and that he was his own agent. Gurcharan informed Om that he had spent the last few years working in England and that he was looking to purchase land in India. The intention, he told him, was to build a family home to move into.

Om's eyes lit up, not just at the prospect of Gurcharan being a potential customer, but a customer who was working in a foreign country, which meant potential new leads.

Bubbling with excitement, Om swiftly sipped his cup of tea and invited Gurcharan to accompany him on some viewings. They both spent the rest of the day together, with Om guiding Gurcharan through the process of purchasing. It resulted into a fruitful exercise as the following day Gurcharan saw a plot he liked which had a purchase value of 12,000 Rupees. There was no negotiation required, as it was a good price and Om Prakash spent the next few days getting the deal completed.

Gurcharan discussed this with Inder who supported the decision and collectively they parted with the deposit to purchase the land. It was only when Om Prakash called Gurcharan to confirm all the paperwork was complete, that both the brothers decided to break the news to their parents.

Instead of being happy at this new prospect, anxious faces stared back at Inder and Gurcharan. Surjan Singh took them both aside and expressed his concern at the expense that was involved in building a house. He wanted to be sure that his sons were aware of the commitment.

If there was any seed of doubt, he wanted to know, as they could still pull out of the deal. This was their hard-earned money they were now investing, and it had to be successful as the whole family depended on it. Without a hint of regret, or concern, the brothers provided further reassurance to their father that the plot had been purchased and he needn't worry about the build costs or completion. Deep inside, Inder and Gurcharan knew only too well the risks their siblings had taken to support their own move to England.

The mood changed as details were shared about the build of their new house. It would be three storeys high and split into five equal portions, one for each member of the family. Surjan Singh was taken aback by the conversation. In his admission Inder and Gurcharan were funding the whole build, and so they should have larger portions to themselves, with smaller sharing quarters for the other siblings. However, Inder insisted it was only fair to apportion as planned.

Inder spoke on behalf of Gurcharan when he reminded them of their support and courage and how instrumental everyone had been with regards to England. Just because they had lived and worked in a foreign country, their roots were firmly fixed to the homeland and the family.

The acquisition of land for the new house was only one part of the objective. Seeing that Gurcharan was on extended stay in India, he had the small matter of marriage. There was much catching up to do with Charanjit, as she had remained exceptionally patient, and her frequent correspondences kept her future husband motivated. No longer would they meet under the strict supervision of extended family. The trust earned over the last two years was unquestionable.

With the arrival of December came the wedding. Gurcharan was now a young man with added responsibility. The month also signalled time to go back to England and re-join his place of work. Charanjit wouldn't be travelling back until better arrangements were made.

Inder had planned on travelling back soon after but the current situation put this on hold. With them both back in England there was a risk the building of the house may never get off the ground. Many days were spent discussing the best course of action. The build project could be left with family members, but what if they ran into problems? How challenging would it be to manage proceedings, and make decisions while in England? It was important not to lose any momentum.

After much debate, Inder took it upon himself to remain in India and oversee the build of the foundations and outer structure. Although this provided Gurcharan with much needed assurance, it also saddened him that Inder would almost certainly lose his job. But in the grand scheme of things, the project was much more important to them and Inder was certain another opportunity in England would reveal itself in time.

Search for a partner starts

It was the day of Gurcharan's flight back to England and that very morning, both he and Inder travelled to Sis Ganj Gurdwara[20] to take blessings for a safe flight. On their way back to the car park, Gurcharan once again bumped into an old school friend by the name of Bhupinder Singh. Hugs were exchanged and old times recalled, with Gurcharan telling him of his recent meeting with Om Prakash.

Time was short and Gurcharan was disappointed they couldn't talk more. Bhupinder briefly mentioned that he was looking for a prospective match for his sister, Diljeet, and that if Gurcharan knew of anyone suitable then to let him know.

Without a moment's hesitation Gurcharan told Bhupinder that such a match was closer than he

---

[20] Sikh Holy place of worship located in Delhi. It was constructed in 1783 to commemorate the martyrdom site of the ninth Sikh Guru, Guru Tegh Bahadur Ji.

thought. It so happened that his family were also looking for a suitable partner for Inder, and that it would be a good idea for the two of them to meet. Exchanging details Gurcharan left for England, thus leaving it in the capable hands of his sister to follow up the potential marriage opportunity for Inder.

No sooner had Gurcharan touched down in Heathrow that their sister acted on her new mission. The drive to Chandigarh took a couple of hours, and it was only Inder and his sister Swarn Kaur travelling to meet Diljeet and her family. Arriving at the house, Inder sat nervously on the tired looking armchair while Swarn Kaur exchanged family backgrounds with Diljeet's parents. She wasted no time in proudly mentioning that Inder had been working in England for a few years now, and that the brothers were building a new house not far from here.

Diljeet's entry triggered a momentary glance from Inder, she was dressed in a pale-yellow salwar kameez, with head bowed and not once acknowledging his presence. They were both left alone for a while to have a conversation however, much of it was one-sided and this somewhat disheartened Inder. His expectation was someone a bit more modern, a trait stipulated from his time spent in England while mixing with different people. Had he not lived in England he may not have been so fussy. In his estimation, he wasn't being arrogant, it was just that he knew what he wanted.

The conversation lasted for a short while and a despondent Inder respectively thanked the family and requested leave, promising to share his decision soon. His silence on the way home was proof enough for his sister that the meeting hadn't gone well. She never pushed for an answer but took it upon herself to inform Diljeet's family. For now, Inder's search continued in amongst the build of the new house.

But his parents remained hot on his heels with prospective match making and this latest bout was about to prove a success. Having met a girl from Delhi, they had seemed to click and a few meetings later all seemed on course for marriage. Everything had been agreed and a date for the wedding finally fixed.

News filtered to Inder's uncle, Surjan Singh's eldest brother about the wedding. He then enquired about the family's background and their caste. This was something Inder didn't care about, but this modern thinking still had some catching up to do with the extended family.

Some things are just meant to be

There was hope in the family that the turn of the year would bring more wedding celebrations in the house. Inder was still in India and his engagement was on the horizon. Gurcharan arrived a day before to be part of the auspicious occasion. He was also pleased that the build work was well underway but disappointed that Inder's potential match with Bhupinder's sister failed to materialise.

Gurcharan told Inder about the welcome and praise he received when he got back to England. Everyone had been so proud of their achievement with regards to the road trip. Some of their friends were so inspired that even they were considering a road trip of their own. The only disappointment was that no pictures had been taken to show the countries they passed through. Inder agreed that in hindsight they should have purchased a camera, even if it was with monetary help from friends. While they had no photos, the memory of each mile of the road was etched in their minds forever.

Preparations ahead of the engagement were all in place however, Surjan Singh was worried he hadn't heard anything from his elder brother. He consulted with Inder and Gurcharan as to what the reason could be and whether he was attending the ceremony after all.

Inder struggled to sleep on the eve of his engagement, with a mixture of excitement and trepidation churning in his stomach. Gurcharan was much the same but that was the jet lag playing havoc. His body clock was now well tuned to the shores of England.

The sounds of the morning birds chirping together with beeping horns almost drowned out the shouting coming from outside the house. As Inder listened carefully, he could hear his father's name being bellowed out. As family members gathered, Gurcharan peered outside and spotted his father's older brother walking angrily towards the house. He was shouting all sorts of things, and he threatened Surjan Singh that if he didn't come outside, he would rip down the door and drag him out.

Panic now engulfed every bone in Inder's body. It was his big day and there was too much commotion unfolding outside. Plucking up the courage, he walked out to see if he could bring some calm to what was sure to turn into a riot.

Surjan Singh's elder brother was a very strict man and of fierce nature whose annoyance was spread across his face. Obviously pleased to see Inder, he calmed down and went about explaining his frustration. His main gripe was that no one had bothered delving into the background of the family Inder was marrying into. They were of a different caste and such unions had never taken place in the family before. Such disregard angered Surjan Singh's elder brother and he couldn't understand why this marriage was going ahead.

Finally stepping inside, he confronted his brother while everyone watched on. Surjan Singh kept quiet the whole time and didn't dare speak up against his brother. Inder's hopes of marriage evaporated when it was decided no one would travel to Delhi. Then came the final blow as Surjan Singh's brother picked up the phone and rang the family, telling them there had been a big misunderstanding and there would be no engagement. It ended with a Panjabi salutation and slamming of the phone. No one dared challenge this decision, and a dejected Inder walked back to his room and shut the door behind him. He wished he was back in England right now.

Inder was sitting more comfortably on the single armchair in Chandigarh, waiting for Diljeet to come in with a tray of tea and snacks. It was a low-key and intimate affair and Inder had realised he had been too hasty in his observations of Diljeet the first time. Her shyness was a perfect example of her calm nature, something he would come to appreciate for many years.

With the foundations of his long-term future cemented, so too were the foundations of their new house complete to allow the build to get underway.

Now he had one more important mission to complete for a dear friend.

Mission complete

The 90km journey to Ludhiana took Inder a couple of hours. This was his first time to Panjab's largest city. The temperature was nearing 40°C as Inder scanned the area until he found the colony he was looking for. The house in this colony belonged to the parents of his friend Jagthar, who he visited in Switzerland during the road trip. Before Inder left Switzerland, Jagthar had taken him aside to confide in him, and to deliver a message.

Inder gingerly knocked on the door, hoping someone would open it as he hadn't notified the family in advance. The elderly man was Jagthar's father, he recalled the face from a photo he'd been shown.

Inder introduced himself and was welcomed in for some tea. Jagthar's parents hadn't heard from their son in almost two years and were very worried about his well-being. On advice from Jagthar, Inder delivered the required message. He told them that their son, after a shaky start had now established himself well in Europe. Unlike some who had remained in one place, their son had managed to travel around Europe while working successfully job to job.

He understood they were concerned but that they remain patient, for he was doing fine having met him recently. Inder then handed over an envelope which contained some money, **a small token of your son's hard work** Inder commented.

Inder didn't stay too long and was grateful for the hospitality shown. They now looked as if a burden had been removed from their shoulders. He promised he would contact Jagthar very soon and to ask him to call them on a regular basis. With that, he requested leave and made his way back to the train station for his journey home.

Now seated in the musky cabin, Inder removed a sealed envelope from his jacket. On the front Jagthar had written the words *Pyraeh Phitta Aur Maata* (beloved father and mother). At the time of handing this over, Jagthar mentioned that he'd written of his shame of failing to establish a job, and for his lack of will power to be persistent. That he was afraid of telling his parents the truth of his plight thus risking breaking their hearts. That was the only thing Jagthar had given him that day to take on his journey back home. Inder folded the sealed envelope and put it back into his pocket.

Inder remained in India for a total of seven months after the road trip, to oversee the completion of the construction. Most of the work was funded by money Inder and Gurcharan had transferred back home. By the time Inder returned to England in the autumn, all external build work was complete.

Thereafter, the brothers sent the equivalent of 15,000 Rupees a month to ensure work continued. Each month, and without delay, they would receive a letter from home which included an update on the build with the odd picture to warm their hearts.

Beyond the Road

It was 1969 and the brothers were still renting the same house on Petersfield Avenue in Slough. Both had good jobs that paid well and so they felt now was the right time to take steps to make England their permanent residence. The necessary paperwork was initiated and well in progress when they received a letter from their father.

The letter was short as their father was a man of very few words. But these particular words signalled the achievement of their eventual dream. Reading it carefully, their father made a humble request to stop sending money for the house. When Gurcharan read the words, *all work has been completed*, he could have been forgiven for letting the tears flow down his cheeks.

Their father instructed them that it was time to save for their future, and to start thinking about themselves. These words made the hardship and sacrifice of the last few years so worthwhile. Inder and Gurcharan's parents were now the proud owners of their own house. Even Inder couldn't contain his emotions and the brothers hugged in celebration. With the family better established, it was time to make another trip home and bring over their respective wives to England.

Their stay in India was brief, and included surveying the new house while making the necessary preparations for their partners to fly back. Inder took the opportunity to spend a few days with his sister at her marriage home in Chandigarh. It was mid-afternoon when Inder boarded his bus to go back to Hoshiarpur. The bus was not that busy, so Inder decided to walk to the back where he intended to stretch across the back seats and close his eyes.

As he walked through the isle, he caught a glimpse of a face he had seen before. Inder didn't stop but continued to the end of the bus. He kept his eyes fixed on the person he had recognised however, the woman didn't turn around. He was now certain the woman in question was Sarita, Roy's wife.

Before the bus got going, Inder bravely walked back down to where Sarita was sitting, with a view of just saying hello. Sarita was surprised but pleased to see Inder and requested that he sit in the vacant seat next to her.

Inder told Sarita about the new house they had built for the family and of his marriage. They spoke at length about the road trip, and how fortunate they had all been to come away intact, even after the close run-in with the police.

He didn't want to infringe on Sarita's privacy, so casually asked about the rest of the family. Sarita was aware that Roy had spoken to him and Gurcharan about their situation, at which Inder blushed. She went on to explain they had faced intense days of debating and consoling upon arrival to their respective homes.

Eloping to another country was still fresh in the minds of their parents. This was further escalated by the revelation that Kunal had been conceived outside of wedlock. The whole process had been draining on them and so they spent a few weeks in Shimla with friends, to get a much-needed break.

But it seemed Kunal had melted the hearts of his grandparents. He was the first grandchild in both the respective families. On returning from Shimla they remained at Roy's parents' house, the mood had now changed, and they were all on the path of forgiveness and acceptance.

Inder was keen to know what happened to the car and Sarita soon relieved his fears. Roy left nothing to chance and exchanged details with one of the Sardars while they were in Kabul. The car never made it to India but was transported back to England.

Roy had realised there was no need to use the car to prove their success, for Kunal was their biggest achievement. An authorised dealership had taken the car in for essential repairs, who warned Roy it wouldn't be cheap however, he wanted that car restored to its original state wherever possible.

Inder mentioned that he was sad they never exchanged details when they had arrived two years ago but that he understood the reason. The Chauhan family needed space and time with their families to repair burnt bridges.

Sarita commented they were no longer living in Slough and had moved to Reading. Inder nodded in approval but never pushed for contact details or the mention of meeting up. He was happy that things had worked out for the three of them and the future looked more positive.

Time flew by in discussions and very soon Sarita's stop arrived. Before getting off the bus, Inder handed Sarita some money by way of a gift for Kunal. She didn't refuse the kind gesture as she knew the brothers had grown fond of Kunal during the road trip. They both wished each other the best for the future. Inder hoped that one day their paths would cross back in England.

Firmly cemented in England

No sooner had Inder, Gurcharan and their respective wives touched down in England that they were consumed by the news related to events unfolding in Wolverhampton. Reports claimed pressure was mounting on the Wolverhampton Transport Committee regarding the turban incident involving Tarsem Singh Sandhu.

Since the row in 1967, the Committee had stood firm in their stance, with strong backing from a local MP by the name of Enoch Powell. This was a man who a year earlier had described the turban dispute as *a cloud no bigger than a man's hand that can so rapidly overcast the sky*[21]. While Enoch Powell was sacked as MP following his infamous *River of Blood* speech, his words had the impact he was hoping for.

---

[21] https://www.bbc.co.uk/news/uk-england-birmingham-47853718

In the standoff, Mr Sohan Singh Jolly (UK president of the principal Sikh political party of Panjab) retaliated, setting down a deadline that if the ban was not reversed by 30th April, he would burn himself alive. As the deadline loomed, and with no sign of Mr Jolly backing down, the Committee became increasingly nervous. Therefore, on 9th April 1969, the ban was lifted, allowing Tarsem Singh Sandhu to return to work with a beard and turban.

This change in law was a momentous victory for those who wanted to maintain their articles of faith and practice their religion. It was a proud moment for Inder and Gurcharan who like so many others benefitted from the collective efforts of a brave few.

The brothers remained in Slough and continued to apply themselves diligently in work and home life. But their experiences on the road taught them many new things, namely that they wanted to do something for themselves.

Inder was the first to venture out onto new horizons. He had a friend in Slough called Mr Kalra who worked in the insurance industry. Realising a potential opportunity to learn a new skill, a series of meetings were arranged for Inder to work alongside Mr Kalra. The learning curve was fast and Inder was willing to absorb all the information that could be thrown at him.

When Mr Kalra was confident of Inder's ability, he advised him to open an office in Gravesend. With the support of his friend, Inder successfully started his insurance business in a small office on Harmer Street in 1971. This was a major step as for the first time, Inder had stepped away from his comfort zone to now run his own business. By 1975, he had two children no older than five and together with Diljeet began the journey to settle in the town of Gravesend.

Gurcharan remained in Slough and had a strong bond with his employer. This was the main reason he was able to retain his job following the road trip and subsequent trips to India. However, the fortunes of Fred Mayer changed as they were taken over by an American company called Barlow Handling in 1975.

Their expansion policy included the purchasing of a new site, an airfield hanger in Maidenhead.

As the company grew and recruited more workers, Gurcharan benefitted from increased responsibility. Within a year of the new premises opening, he was promoted to assistant manager and responsible for a team of field engineers. He was the only Indian person still employed and was now managing a team of fifteen people.

Gurcharan's home responsibilities had also increased as by the late 1970s he had two children of his own and often took them to work because of childcare constraints.

While working at Barlow Handling, Gurcharan set himself up as a driving instructor in 1976. The additional income proved lucrative enough and so on advice from his brother, Inder followed suit by operating as a driving instructor in Gravesend. But the brothers never settled for the norm. They were risk takers and confident in their abilities to try their hand at new things.

Gurcharan eventually moved his driving business to Gravesend, and for a while travelled from Slough each day to give lessons. Enjoying the fruits of their new ventures, they took a major step towards expansion and in 1977 purchased a shop on Pelham Road in Gravesend. The intention was to operate their insurance broker business while maintaining the driving however, they soon became stuck.

The owner of the business next door, a butcher's shop, refused the request posted by the local council. Not having permission, this left Inder and Gurcharan in an awkward situation. They had a shop for which they were paying rent but unable to use it for their chosen business.

A close friend presented the brothers with a possible solution. He had a way where they could still practice the insurance business and use the shop to generate income. But for this they would have to invest in stock, this being electrical goods.

The main part of the shop would be used for the sale of electrical items, and just a few to understand the level of interest. Kettles and toasters were the first items to make it into the shop window. The brothers continued their insurance business from the back office and were relaxed even if they didn't sell any electrical items. However, within a matter of days all the items were purchased by local customers, and they were left with no stock against rising demand.

Realising a potential opportunity, Gurcharan decided they take a gamble and place a larger order of kettles, toasters and some Russian manufactured radios. The unique thing about these radios was they were able to pick up European and Indian channels, which conventional radios were unable to do so.

Within no time, the radios flew off the shelves and were a great hit with the growing Indian community in Gravesend. Then Inder noticed an advert in the local newspaper showing an item called a VHS recorder. This device allowed people to watch movies on it. Better still, you could record a programme from TV onto a VHS tape and watch it as many times as you liked.

Inder asked around the local community about the VHS recorder, which seemed the talk of the town, but very few people had one. While they were expensive, this wasn't the main hinderance to not buying one. The problem was that it was difficult to acquire blank VHS tapes for recording.

Sensing an opportunity, Inder decided they invest in a handful of blank tapes. Once again, as soon as they made their way onto the shelves, customers were flocking in to purchase them. The entire stock was sold within a matter of days. Seeing the surge in popularity, they decided to take a chance and purchased the actual video recorder.

Two days later a customer walked into their shop and purchased one for £600. Their half-hearted journey into the business world had been a whirlwind which turned into an established electrical business within twelve months.

Confidence grew, and with it they purchased more stock, became regular distributers and achieved better discounts with major suppliers and manufacturers. In the space of five years, the brothers had expanded once again, and now operated a total of three electrical shops across Gravesend and Bexleyheath. Their insurance business continued to flourish and as driving instructors they were the preferred choice for first generation Indians who wanted to drive but found language a barrier.

Inder and Gurcharan went on to run successful businesses and became an integral part of the local community. Inder later served as Justice of the Peace for twenty years, and both tirelessly supported multiple charities.

Looking back, and at a time when many first-generation Indians were settling for manual jobs, Inder and Gurcharan were thinking progression. They were using their skills and background to not only enhance their own lifestyle, but to also share the knowledge of their successes with friends and family.

Epilogue

There is a popular saying that ***behind every successful man, there is a strong woman***. It was my intention to talk about Diljeet and Charanjit in the closing section of this book. Importantly, I didn't want their support and contributions to get lost amongst the great adventures that Inder and Gurcharan experienced.

It was Charanjit's patience and strong belief during the early period of their engagement that kept Gurcharan motivated in England. After an unsuccessful first meeting, it was Diljeet who was prepared to see Inder a second time for future marriage. Her calming influence and support were a major help to Inder during the crucial period of the build of the family home near Chandigarh.

Back in England, when the brothers worked to establish their business, it was Diljeet and Charanjit who spurred them on and became the backbone of the family. Amongst taking care of the children and completing household chores, they were ever present to listen to the day's successes or failures.

Their commitment in helping their husbands was a major factor in the expansion of the electrical business. On days when the brothers were partaking in their driving duties, Charanjit and Diljeet would each manage the respective shops in Gravesend and Bexleyheath. They became the cornerstone for success and continued to do so for over thirty years.

Inder and Gurcharan set foot at Amritsar Airport, in one piece and to the relief of their family after their epic road trip. In all the happiness and celebrating, when Inder and Gurcharan finally met their families, they had travelled some 8000 miles across nine countries. I asked them whether they were disappointed not to have driven all the way to India, and they weren't. The overriding danger to their lives had they attempted was just not worth the risk.

The road trip was a once in a lifetime adventure and an opportunity which may not have presented itself ever again. As they both told their story, I drew on an observation that this experience really helped them shape the future for when they returned to England.

It is no coincidence that this was a contributing factor for them to go on and achieve so much success, both in their family life and the wider community. To this day they remained very modest individuals and never openly bragged about this experience or impact, but I know they wouldn't disagree with me.

When I had finished jotting down the main facts about their journey, I asked respected Inder and Gurcharan Singh Chhatwal for some final words.

"We were young, adventurous, we had to go, we can't explain how we felt but had to see these countries, it was a great opportunity. We will never forget this timeline in our lives, yes, we had a huge

amount of luck along the way. Besides the money incident in Paris, the car accident and the unfortunate camel we still feel something was protecting us. But there are two important things you need to know. First that in those days people were very sincere and helpful, we all trusted each other. So, if we stopped anywhere, strangers were willing to point us in the right direction, give us good advice. Secondly, there was more love back then and people opened their hearts to us. This was reflected in the hospitality we felt when we stayed at people's houses, it was overwhelming".

To this day, Inder and Gurcharan never re-acquainted themselves with the Chauhan family when they got back to Slough. Wherever they are today, I am sure they will forever hold gratitude for the two Singh brothers who answered their call and safely drove them along complex terrain in a Morris Austin Cambridge Estate.

Acknowledgments

In Early 2017 tragic news came knocking on our doors. Respected Inder Singh Chhatwal departed this world, leaving us all to ponder the fairness of life. This book is dedicated to his lasting memory and to his brother Gurcharan Singh Chhatwal, who before and after, has been a guiding light and source of inspiration to me. To both the families who I love dearly, I hope the words do justice to their amazing journeys in life.

My thanks to the entire Chhatwal family cannot be summed up in words but they will no doubt know how indebted I am to them. Late Inder Singh Chhatwal and respected Gurcharan Singh Chhatwal for trusting me with their personal and treasured memories. From the very first draft of the manuscript back in 2016 they've been a guiding light every step of the way. The countless interviews, phone calls, reading multiple iterations of the manuscript, they never once turned me down. It is your adventure that gave home to the writer inside me. To Bob, Kiran, Dimple and Renu, your parents are truly inspiring.

I would also like to extend my thanks to Gravesend Library and staff who pointed me in the right direction when I was hitting a brick wall in terms of research. To John Carter (previously a TV presenter of the travel show 'Wish You Were Here', and with over 30 years' experience in the industry) who so diligently took the time to meet me and lend me his prized collection of travel books for research.

My long list of readers who took time out from their busy lives to read my drafts and provide constructive feedback. When I felt the first serious version of the draft was ready, some brave souls stepped forward to read it and provide their feedback. Thanks to my sister Ravleen Beeston, Amarbeer Gill, Kalwinder Dhindsa (author of *My Father & The Lost Legend of Pear Tree*), Yvonne Beeston (self-published author), Sukh Sall and Ritu Bhathal (author of *Marriage Unarranged*).

To Bob Chhatwal for his honest opinions and sharp critique on the manuscript. His contribution to one of the chapters when Inder Singh first lands in England. Then for taking on the task of re-shaping the blurb for this book, which I am so pleased with.

As the manuscript neared completion, I decided to send it out for another round of feedback in January 2020. Once again, I encouraged my readers not to hold back, these braves souls stepped forward to dedicate their time. Kellie Mills, I remember sitting in the small gym office discussing your feedback in between classes. Much travelled Rupinder Sodhi and published author of *The Magic Pearl Necklace* Simrit Bharaj.

Special thanks to my designer Hyde Panesar who translated the essence of this book perfectly to create a nostalgic book cover that I fell in love with the moment I saw it.

Finally, my wife and two children. It was December morning in 2016 when I was running around like a headless chicken preparing for the arrival of Inder and Gurcharan Singh Chhatwal. In the background, almost without any fuss my wife was busily preparing snacks and drinks. Throughout my writing journey that's the very phase that sticks with me, ***without any fuss***, and that is my wonderful wife. When I took the first steps into the manuscript, her encouragement pushed me along. At times when I felt overwhelmed and sometimes frustrated it was her patience and advice that helped clear the mist and help me march on. Continuously I questioned my writing, the very words, doubted the quality, felt unsure as a writer but it was my wife who instilled confidence in me at those challenging times of self-doubt. When the finishing line felt further away, it was she who grabbed me by the hand and pushed me over it. To my wife, Jyoti, to who I'm forever indebted. Not forgetting my two darlings, Rajan and Manav, who so patiently have seen their father engrossed in writing, editing, re-editing, and never walked away from listening to my snippets and ideas.

Thank You All.

Timeline

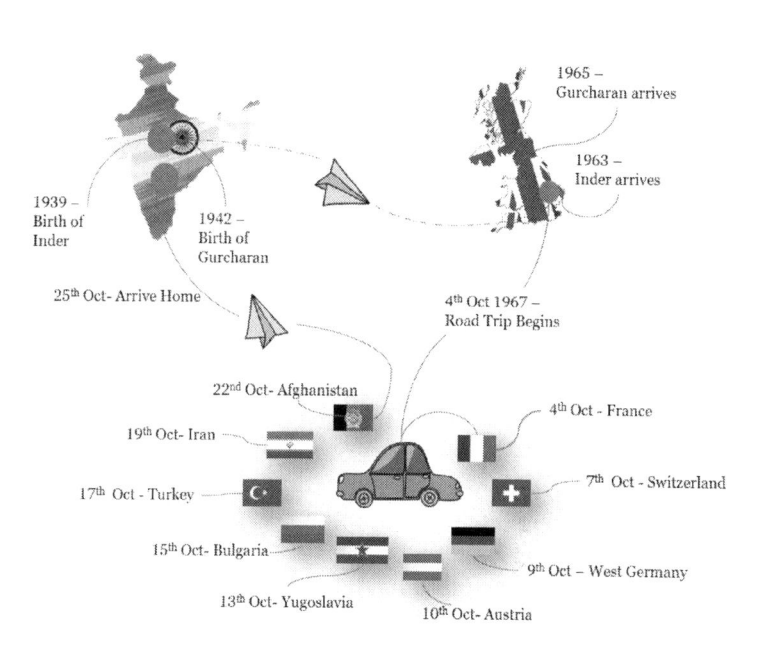

1939 – Birth of Inder
1942 – Birth of Gurcharan
1963 – Inder arrives
1965 – Gurcharan arrives
4th Oct 1967 – Road Trip Begins
4th Oct - France
7th Oct - Switzerland
9th Oct – West Germany
10th Oct - Austria
13th Oct - Yugoslavia
15th Oct - Bulgaria
17th Oct - Turkey
19th Oct - Iran
22nd Oct - Afghanistan
25th Oct - Arrive Home

Inder's Voucher for England

MINISTRY OF LABOUR
VOUCHER
Ref. No. 030304 N
Issued for the purposes of Section 2 of the COMMONWEALTH IMMIGRANTS ACT, 1962

14 AUG 1963

Voucher N° 045410   Date of Expiry 6th August, 1963.

See Extension Overleaf

Full Name .... CHHATWAL, INDER SINGH
Address .... FIELD DIVISION I.B. PUNJAB, NANGAL TOWN-SHIP, DIST. HOSHIARPUR, PUNJAB, INDIA.
Date of Birth 30.8.1939. Sex M/F Country of Birth INDIA
Occupation .... DRAUGHTSMAN (MECH.)
Passport No. ——— Country of issue of passport ———

NOTES

1. This voucher must be produced together with a valid passport to the Immigration Officer at the port of arrival in the United Kingdom. Failure to produce it may result in refusal of admission.
2. This voucher may be presented only by the person described therein.
3. This voucher cannot be used for entry to the United Kingdom after the date of expiry shown above, unless an extension has been granted. It does not entitle the holder to take work in Northern Ireland.

Signed on behalf of the Minister of Labour

Date 7th February, 1963.

E.D. 413

Morris Austin Cambridge Estate

A similar model to the one pictured above was used for the road trip in 1967.

Image created by Simon GP Geoghegan

Gurdwara on 79 Sinclair Road, Shepherd Bush

This is the Gurdwara that Inder and Gurcharan Singh Chhatwal used to visit every Sunday when residing in the UK

Source :
https://hammersmithfulhamforum.com/2016/11/21/the-sikh-sacrifice-for-british-freedom/

Gurcharan and Charanjit with family

From left to right: Paramjit (young brother), Surjan Singh (father), Permeshri Kaur (Mother), Karthar Singh (brother), Charanjit (Gurcharan's wife), Gurcharan Singh himself.

Happy couples

From left to right: Inder, Diljeet, Charanjit, Gurcharan

Returning home after the road trip

Food being prepared as part of the Akand Paath ceremony for when Inder and Gurcharan reached India after road trip

Petersfield Avenue

After Gurcharan arrived in England in 1965, the brothers decided to move out from Chanan Singh's house and rented this house in Petersfield Avenue before eventually moving to Gravesend.

Late Inder Singh Chhatwal

Bibliography

Slough Observer – Slough Library, UK

Slough History Online -sloughhistoryonline.org

Blue Guide Austria by Ian Robertson

Blue Guide Western Germany by James Bentley 2nd Edition

The Companion Guide to Jugoslavia by J.A.Cuddon

Blue guide – Turkey – The Aegean and Mediterranean Coasts 1st Edition – Bernard Mc Donagh

Special Thanks to:

John Carter – Presenter of BBC's *Holiday* programme and ITV's *Wish You Were Here*

Gravesend Library

About the Author

Apinder Sahni was born in Wolverhampton in the mid-1970s, but before he even had a chance to sample the local culture his family moved to Kent. His parents were born in Iran and grew up during its Western period, later moving to India. Eventually their destiny brought them to England and as many other immigrants, they began a challenging journey.

Growing up he always enjoyed writing. Whether it was short horror stories or adventures in space, he'd be seen busily scribbling something. The transition to sharing his stories publicly on a personal blog came after he attended a family wedding in 2010. Ten years on he is pleased to still be active on the blogging scene with a loyal following.

Now a self-confessed notebook geek, he has reams of pages with short stories and observations inspired by his family and the world around him.

Apinder lives with his wife and two children in Kent. He loves cycling, sharing the cooking at home and watching his kids play football. He is also a lifelong Liverpool FC fan and pleased they won the Premier League title in his lifetime. Sometimes, you can find him hosting and performing comedy across the UK with his duo as The ChuckleSinghs.

The Amazing Road Trip Home – England to India With Strangers is his first book.

Printed in Great Britain
by Amazon